THE ROGUE'S MOON

ROBERT W. CHAMBERS

Stark House Press • Eureka California

THE ROGUE'S MOON

Published by Stark House Press
1315 H Street
Eureka, CA 95501, USA
griffinskye3@sbcglobal.net
www.starkhousepress.com

THE ROGUE'S MOON

ISBN: 979-8-88601-107-4

Cover design by Jeff Vorzimmer, ¡caliente!design, Austin, Texas
Cover art by James Gale Tyler
Book design by Mark Shepard, shepgraphics.com
Proofreading by Bill Kelly

PUBLISHER'S NOTE

First Stark House Press Edition: April 2024

The Rogue's Moon

"Vastly atmospheric, with lots of interesting period details… The story throws every famous pirate of the era together into a wild ride, plus romance, danger and buried treasure. Great fun."—Amazon reader

"One of Chambers' most gloriously sumptuous potboilers. Loaded with overblown romance and swashbuckling pirates, this one is a plum of the early 20th century high end pulp adventures."
— Julie Maruskin

"Chambers captures the spirit and sensibilities of the period."—Bill Kelly

"Mr. Chambers has an original creative imagination of great power…. a master of natural dialogue, a strong, picturesque descriptive writer, and the possessor of a keen sense of humor."—*N.Y. Press*

"The most imaginative and fantastic romances must have their basis in real life."
—Robert W. Chambers, from an interview

FOREWORD

The east coast of North America was infested by pirates when the Colonies were young.

These sea-wolves roamed singly or in packs along the lanes of trade. They came into harbours and took merchant vessels under the noses of enraged governors and horrified citizens.

Sometimes they landed and laid a port under contribution. Charleston, South Carolina, was served in this fashion by that beguiling sea-saunterer, Mr. Teach, sometimes known as Black-Beard.

Between the years 1690 and 1720 there were more than two thousand pirates afloat off our coasts between Maine and Florida.

On New Providence Island, in the Bahamas, and dreadfully convenient to our coast, nearly two thousand more of this sea gentry loafed about to acknowledge the Royal Proclamation, accept the King's pardon, go to sea again in pretense of honest privateering, turn pirate once more at the first opportunity, and end, often, on Execution Dock.

It was almost as much as a skipper's life was worth to trade along the Atlantic coast. Everywhere some sea-rogue or other lurked to take incoming or outgoing vessels.

The Royal Navy maintained station-ships in the West Indies and along our coasts—a kind of marine police—and in some measure these warships and their tenders checked the ever-increasing piracy threatening total extinction of some of the American Colonies.

This, then, was the situation confronting the seaboard population of America in 1700. New York City had become a stench in the nostrils of England, and was called a pirate's nest.

Virginia named the Albemarle Colony, in Carolina, "Rogue's Bay."

The coasts of the Carolinas and Virginia were peculiarly adapted to the uses of pirates where were so many inlets, sounds, bays, creeks—all good lurking places and good refuges if chased by superior forces.

Also, here pirates could careen and clean their vessels, often undiscovered, usually unmolested.

Now in regard to the historic characters which appear in "The Rogue's Moon" stories: the majority are not imaginary but real, and so are the episodes concerning them.

No liberties have been taken with facts, nor has history been consciously violated in these stories.

Upon one or two matters the author has permitted himself to speculate—for example, upon the fate of Mr. Francis Farrington Sprigg, whose terminal history remains a mystery.

Mary Read, a girl pirate, really appears to have been the generous, courageous, and chaste character presented. The duel she fought, and the motive for fighting it, are historically correct.

The character of the other female pirate, Anne Bonny, has been drawn without prejudice. It was said of her that she was not only unable to remain faithful to her latest lover but that she couldn't even remain so to a whole ship's company. Her cold-blooded remark to John Rackham, known as Calico Jack, a few moments before he was hanged for piracy, is fact, not fiction.

Black-Beard's real name was Drummond. He was a filthy creature—no crueller, perhaps, than Ned Low and Francis Farrington Sprigg—but morally viler. He called himself Edward Thatch, which often was written "Teach."

Tom Cocklyn met his fate as indicated. Poor Stede Bonnet faced his fate less courageously at the end. Why he was not sent to England for trial, as Lieutenant Rhett advised—offering, even, to go with the wretched major—nobody seems to know. He should have been examined in lunacy.

Israel Horneygold was supposed to be brother to the pirate Horneygold who turned pirate-chaser.

The young man, John Ross, who figures largely in these stories, is supposed to be the youngest son of Lord Cardross who went to Port Royal in 1683.

Nancy Topsfield is a created character.

In regard to the Honourable Charles Eden, Governor of North Carolina, opinions differ. He made an excellent Governor; and if, in a moment of weakness, he trafficked unlawfully with pirates, he paid a terrible price for it in the end.

His Secretary, Knight, seems to have been on unholy terms with Black-Beard, anyway. And of one thing there is no doubt; the general belief was that both Governor and Secretary were in league with pirates; and that is why the merchants and planters of North Carolina sent to Governor Spottswood, of Virginia, for help against pirates, and did not run to their own Governor Eden.

Few people in these days realize how terrible a war was waged in the Carolinas between the infant Colonies and the Tuscaroras.

The Tuscarora, or Essaurora, Indians were part of the Iroquois nation—the most virile and merciless warriors in North America.

This war was practically at an end at the time the action begins in these stories, and it is merely mentioned.

But until the Tuscarora, finally, marched northward to join the Five Nations in New York Colony, and change their federated title to that of "The Six Nations," there was no safety for the whites in the Carolinas, and little, even, in Virginia.

Districts most frequented by pirates lay along the coast between Cape Fear and the Virginia Capes.

Topsail Inlet, where much of the action in these stories takes place, was a notorious rendezvous for sea-rogues. Here they came to careen, or for water, for provisions, or to revel and generally misbehave.

Here the talented Mr. Teach played his dirtiest trick on his fellow rogues, and left a couple of dozen of them, later, to suck their thumbs on a maroon shore where, by sheerest luck, poor Stede Bonnet found and rescued them.... To little purpose, for the majority were sent to the gallows when Rhett took Stede Bonnet.

Poor Bonnet. His last letters read like letters from a lunatic just awakening to a first glimmer of reason after a long nightmare of insanity.

But, in those days, there were few to care and nobody to inquire whether a man of wealth, position, consequence, and highest respectability, who, utterly ignorant of the sea, suddenly turned pirate, might not possibly be mentally irresponsible.

Earlier, the world sent a guiltless man to the gallows for murder and piracy, who never had committed an act of piracy and who had been known for his bravery, honesty, and domestic virtues—a man of substance, fortune and to whom the City of New York had voted a sum of money in recognition of public virtues.

If, unintentionally, he slew a mutineer, he was absolutely justified.

His name was William Kidd, and he was hanged, innocent, to save the reputations of several noble gentlemen and prominent citizens in America and in England—among whom might be mentioned his Majesty the King, Lord Bellomont, Mr. Livingston, and several of the noble Lords of Trade.

So it is small wonder that, later, they hanged Stede Bonnet, once major in the British Army, and a gentleman of consideration and attainment who, however, scarcely knew the stem from the stern of a ship when he purchased a schooner on the spur of a mad moment and ran up the Black Flag to take all nations.

The life of a fore-mast man and conditions generally in the merchant service in those days were rather shocking. Temptation to turn pirate, therefore, was the stronger; and it really is a wonder that so many ships' crews remained honest.

Yet, piracy usually began—not in the merchant service—but aboard privateers.

Letters of marque and reprisal were rather vague; and the limits set, elastic. It was the easiest thing in the world to stretch such commissions over the borders of piracy, and to begin to take flags representing nations not at war with England and her Colonies.

Of course the Grand Mogul's trade suffered the worst; and whether his Empire was at war or at peace with other nations, the ships of those nations generally considered the Mogul's vessels fair prey.

It was the roar of rage from the Grand Mogul, after the pirate, James Avery, had taken a ship of his with one of his daughters aboard, that loosed the lightning which destroyed Captain Kidd.

For the Mogul swore that unless England made reparation he would destroy every English, French, and Portuguese factory in India and murder the factors. The frightened East India Company ran to the King of England with piteous cries—and, not knowing that Avery was guilty, found it convenient to charge Captain Kidd with the crime. Something in this manner began one of the darkest tragedies that ever disgraced England and America and England's King and Courts of Law.

Contrary to general opinion, the captain of a pirate ship was not an autocrat. Elected, he held his post at the pleasure of his officers and crew, and could be deposed for cause.

The cruellest captains held their positions longest.

Teach occasionally shot up a few of his crew for no other reason, he admitted, than that it was a good thing to do to keep them to their duty.

One crew deposed and degraded its captain because he seemed to be afraid to attack a man-of-war more heavily armed than he.

In action, however, when action once was decided upon in general conference aboard a sea-rover, the captain reigned supreme.

Articles of agreement signed by the crew aboard a pirate are curious documents to read. The death penalty for infringement is frequently mentioned.

It was due to these articles that Mary Read obtained permission to pick a quarrel with, and fight, her opponent aboard Jack Rackham; and her reason for doing it certainly did her credit. Contemporary portraits of this girl, and of Anne Bonny, crudely bear out personal descriptions left by those who knew them.

The description of that able gentleman, Judge Nicholas Trott, comes from Nancy Topsfield, and, therefore, is scarcely reliable.

Governor Johnson, of South Carolina, was the able executive pictured; as was also, of course, the celebrated Governor Spottswood, of Virginia.

It was a strange century in our country, ruthless and picturesque; and who were rogues and who honest folk, ashore or afloat, is often very difficult to decide.

The Lords Proprietors of North Carolina—even through their Palatine and Vice-Palatine—being utterly unable to keep order in the colony and defend and develop it, were presently kicked out, as is well known.

Governor Eden was the first Governor who amounted to anything in the colony. The mystery surrounding this man remains really unsolved.

CHAPTER I
THE SEA-ROGUE'S MOON

Through a crack of the pantry door the guest was visible. He sat in a window corner, elbows on table, face crotched between both hands.

Sunset glow faded in till and taproom. Winds went down with the sun.

Through an open casement behind him came the steady roar of ocean, seeming to grow louder as the still world darkened. Aromatic odours of cinnamon, lime juice, malt; of spirits, of brown sugar, hung heavy in taproom and till, tinctured by freshening fragrance of mounting seas.

After a while the young man turned and closed the window behind him.

"Boy!" he called.

Now I chance to be a girl and no boy; nevertheless I answered him.

"Boy," said he, "fetch a light!"

"Two, sir?"

"No; one."

"Very good, my lord—"

"Why do you call me that!" he said in a startled voice.

"Because you look it, sir—"

"Damnation, I'm Jack Ross; and see to it that you remember!"

I went to the till-shelf and took a candle in a pewter stick. When I had set it aflame from a kitchen coal I carried it to the young man in the taproom. Noticing that his leather jack stood emptied I laid one hand on it, inquiringly.

"Yes," he said, "your New Berne brew again."

"Will you sup, sir?"

"Not yet."

When I returned with the slopping jack he took it from me, blew the foam till it flew like spindrift all over the table.

"Come here, you freckle-faced pup," said he, "and wet your virgin lips like a true man!"

I thanked him, tasted the brew, and set the jack between his spread arms which clutched the table's edges as though he would break the top into two halves.

"How old are you?" said he, a-staring at me as though thinking of something else.

"Seventeen, sir."

"Have you ever been at sea?"

"Yes, sir."

"With Tom Cocklyn, eh? Before he turned honest innkeeper?"

"No, sir."

"I think you lie, you little swipe," said he; "you've sailed already On The Account,* and you know it!"

"Would you make of a young boy an old pirate, sir, because he is servant to Tom Cocklyn of Topsail Inlet?"

"Come," said he, "admit that you've sailed in the Red Sea Trade!"

"Shall I take you, then, for a pirate, sir, because you bait here at The Lost Ship?"

"You had better not," said he, glaring at me out of sea-gray eyes.

After a pause: "A long clay," he said, "and some Charles-Town, scented."

I fetched him a new clay pipe and the Chinese jar of tobacco which was scented with vanilla bean and mixed with orange flowers.

"Will you sup, sir?" I asked again.

"That's twice you ask.... Yes, I will sup when the gentleman I am to meet arrives."

"You say his name is Captain Death?"

"It's spelled that way, but pronounced Deeth.... An old English name, I believe."

---

* *On The Account* and the *Red Sea Trade* were terms for piracy.

"Yes, sir. And when this Captain Death—"

"Deeth, I tell you!"

"Yes, sir.... When he of the ominous name arrives I am to show him into the back parlour and come and notify you, my lord."

"And if you call me 'my lord' but once again, I take the flat of my sword to you. Do you understand that, you girl-faced gaby?"

I told him I understood.

"Then get out," said he, "and leave me in peace."

First I retired to the till and, through the wicket, considered him intently where he sat morose. Then, satisfied, I took a lighted candle from the buttery, went into the hallway and out by the back door to the mews. From the stable, where I had led his hard-run horse an hour ago, I took a lantern faced with green glass. This I lighted; then, covering it with my jerkin flap, I sped with it across the dunes to the edge of the tall pine forest.

There was a dead tree there. Upon a crooked stick I hoisted my lantern and hooked it on a stark limb where it swung, burning with a clear, green light like a flame o' witch-fire above a bog.

When I returned to The Lost Ship Tavern I crept behind the till where, seated upon a high stool, I peered, sometimes through the spindles at the young man by the window, sometimes out at the moon which now was become the Sea-Rogue's Moon, so called, and was full; and drew heavy surf that thundered ceaselessly beyond the inlet.

My meditations were stealthy, dark, and merciless, born of deathless patience. I knew what there was to be done with this young man, but not yet whether I could accomplish it.

I slid off my high stool and went into the kitchen where Herith sat asleep; and roused him and made him mend the fire against the coming of Captain Death.

We had no other guests at Lost Ship Tavern.

As for Tom Cocklyn, my master, and host of this solitary seaside ordinary, he had gone to Edenton in Albemarle, which lies within the Chowan Precinct north of Sound and River; and is the capital of our Proprietary of North Carolina.

He had told me that his business lay with Charles Eden, Esquire, our Governor, concerning the constantly increasing swarm of pirates, of which he said there were more than two thousand cruising now betwixt Cape Breton and Cape Florida.

But Tom Cocklyn usually lied to me, though he did not suspect I knew it; and I wondered where he really had gone, leaving the lonely tavern to me and to Moll Fair the chambermaid, and to our black cook, Herith.

Moll Fair came to the kitchen presently—a yawning young slattern—and a-tying of her dirty apron.

"Freckles," says she, "does that glum young gentleman bed here this night?"

"I know not," said I.

She went into the pantry and took a peep at him.

"A handsome devil," she whispers, "but a sullen one.... You think him a Red Sea Trader or a highwayman out o' Charles-Town, Freckles?"

"Do his business and his good looks concern you?"

She gave my ear a hearty pinch.

"Does not any handsome rascal concern any woman—you freckle-peppered lick-pot? … Draw me a drop o' malt then, there's a pretty rogue—"

"Not a bubble," said I, "and only a pint of small-beer with your supper-crust and cheese—"

She took hold of my ear to pinch it again, then flounced off to the kitchen where, I doubt not, she laid her upon the settle and fell asleep like the very slut she was.

I went into the dark till and looked through the spindles.

The solitary figure in the corner had not stirred. Candlelight cast his distorted shadow on the plaster wall behind him. Through the small, thick window-panes moonlight splintered into a kind of iridescent web across the darkness.

In another web of my own weaving this dozing, unstirring fly was to be caught, perhaps.

As I stood peering in at him who said he had a rendezvous here with a gentleman called Death—and he spoke truer than he knew—he lifted his brooding face and stared around him out of shadow-eyes.

"Boy!" he called harshly.

I ran to him. He commanded a noggin of cold pineapple rum, and bade me line the glass with lime peel and lay a small stem of cinnamon in it.

When I fetched his grog he had thrown himself back on his chair, his spurred and muddy boots extended, his laced riding coat flung wide, showing a flapped, flowered silk vest, and blond lace, and a pair of horse-pistols.

"Boy!"

"Yes, my lord—"

"You whelp, will you bridle your damned mouth!" he interrupted savagely, catching me by the arm in a grip of steel.

"I'm sorry, sir—" I whimpered; but he nearly jerked me off my feet, and I thought he'd crush my arm bones ere he had done with me.

"Damn you for a swipe," he said, "if you call me 'my lord' before Captain Death I'll wring your girl-like neck for you!"

I snivelled.

"Understand this," he added; "I'll not have Captain Death know—I mean, suspect—that I am other than I seem—I mean, other than I am—which is Jack Ross, come to Carolina out of Virginia.... And so into Albemarle, where is the refuge of all mean whites and runaway servants and—ruined men." He gave me another and fiercer shake:

"That's who I am—Jack Ross, gentleman, ruined by gaming.... If you want your curly yellow head knocked off, call me 'my lord' in his presence!"

I said that I never should have called him "my lord," only that he seemed like one of our great folk.

"For whom, then, do you take me, that you blab and chatter of lords and great folk?" he demanded, with a new and uneasy note in his anger.

In my secret mind I thought to myself that somehow, by accident, I had pricked the truth in him, and the explosion revealed it. But I only gaped at him like a gaby.

He looked at me narrowly for a moment or two before his gaze began to soften.

"Come then, my lad," said he, "did I frighten you?"

"Not very greatly, sir."

"Why, that's well. Come, you young rascal, you shall have a pull at my grog. Old Vernon's famous grog. Here's to you, then!"—he drank—"and now, you to me!"—he thrust the glass toward me.

I wet my lips and returned it.

"No stomach, eh? Why, then? You are a tall lad, after all—though slim as a girl. And you have bowels and a heart, have you not? Answer me!"

"I know not what is in my body, sir."

He laughed: "Now I wonder," said he, "what Tom Cocklyn pays you to rub down horses and draw small-beer in this dingy taproom. Eh?"

"Nothing, sir."

"Indentured?"

"Yes, sir."

"To old Tom Cocklyn! How is that, then, you young rogue?"

"Mr. Ross," said I, "my father was Captain of the *Fancy Nancy*, East Indiaman, out of New York for Cadiz.... Two years ago.... Well, he lost his ship one day.... And died of it. So did my mother.... What becomes of destitute children? Is this world tender toward them?"

"Hah!" said he, "why not revenge yourself on the world then?"

"I have no quarrel with the world, sir."

"Why not? I tell you that all men of spirit, whom the world treats scurvily, should quarrel with that same world and take revenge of her."

"How, sir?"

"As I mean to do!"

He sat up with an ugly laugh and laid his hands on the butts of two brass pistols in his belt.

"Tell me," said he, "are you ambitious to become a real man?"

"I do not believe I could become one," said I.

"Nevertheless you shall," said he heartily; "and mend your fortune, as I shall mend mine. Come, you rogue; play the man! What matters a thin and spindle body if the heart be stout?

"Any lad of spirit can learn to use a lighted linstock, or be taught to swing a hanger or fire a pistol! And that's all you need learn to seize that light-o'-love we call Fortune, by her wanton leg and trip her up till she spills a golden harvest out of her dirty smock!" He waved his hand. "Pick up the gold, lad; and that's all there is to it!"

"Mr. Ross," said I, fearfully, "have you ever sailed On The Account?"

"Not yet." He gave me a sharp look, caught my arm again and pulled me into the candlelight. "Look me in the eye," said he, "or I'll murder you!"

I squeaked and made terrified eyes at him.

Said he: "You young buttery rat, I've told you enough to hang me in any other tavern save The Lost Ship. Do you know what a wagging tongue would cost you?"

"A slit gullet, sir," I whimpered.

At that his grim look softened, and presently he laughed again.

"Well, boy," said he, "will you sign a man's articles and sail with Death and me?"

"Whose articles, sir?"

"Captain Death's."

"To take all flags, sir?"

"To take all flags and be damned to them!"

"Would Captain Death sign a boy aboard him for the Red Sea Tr—"

The loud clanging of the tavern doorbell cut my words. I turned, sped through till and pantry, out to the hallway, and unbarred the tavern door.

Two men stood outside. The pot-bellied one—he of the pasty, caved-in face, pipestem legs, and dreadful bulging belly—waddled into the hallway.

"Is Jack Ross here?" he asked in a hoarse and crummy whisper.

"Be pleased to name yourself, sir," said I.

"Tell him Captain Death is arrived."

"Who else, sir?" I looked at the tall, elegant, dandified man who lounged on the doorstep behind him.

"Francis Farrington Sprigg," said he in an affected voice, and sauntered across the threshold.

I looked hard at him, for his was a cruel name in the Carolinas.

He took snuff, then, regarding me with all the disdain and insolence in the world, and dusting his sharp nose with a laced handkerchief that smelled of a thousand roses, he whispered to the other.

"Dinner for three," said Captain Death in a hollow voice.

I led them to the back parlour; fetched a lighted candle to keep them company; ran to the kitchen; awoke Molly Fair and black Herith; and hastened on to the taproom.

"Mr. Ross," said I, "Captain Death is here—"

"Deeth, damn you!"

"—And with him Mr. Francis Farrington Sprigg—"

"Oh.... Bring them here and lay a cloth." He got up and took me by both ears: "If you call me 'my lord' in their presence I'll break every chicken bone in your flimsy body!"

With that he turned me around and gave me a kick which sent me a-spinning.

I returned with Captain Death. Behind him strolled Francis Farrington Sprigg in his silks and laces and high-heeled boots, still a-dusting of his long thin nose with scented snuff out of a golden box.

There was something dreadful to me about Captain Death, who was like a sick man wasted to the bone; and the ghastly skin on his sunken visage revealed the skull's shape underneath.

But what was more frightful was his great bulbous belly and his hollow voice, seeming to burst out from the bony cavern of his ribs, hoarse, horrible.

"Owls, snakes and lizards!" he growled, "if there's still rum in the world let me soak me to the bones! And here," said he, "is Mr. Francis Farrington Sprigg. A very dainty gentleman. Fetch him a plate o' cream and let him lap it!"

He burst into a jarring laugh, shook hands with Jack Ross, and Francis Farrington Sprigg did the like, looking at the young man down his long, pointed nose.

"Pineapple grog for three, boy," said Mr. Ross; and they all sat down together as I went into the till and became busy with limes, sugar and cinnamon.

I could not keep my eyes from Captain Death. He was like a swollen spider; and his candle-cast shadow was like one, wavering on the wall—as though he were a-dancing in his web—which fat spiders sometimes do.

They talked in low voices, all their snouts together, and three slopping glasses under their wet chins.

When Moll Fair laid the cloth, Captain Death caught her and pulled her to his bony knees, but the wench shrieked, tore loose, and ran, and would not again leave the kitchen where she sat with a scared look while I fetched food and drink.

A dish of smoking fish, browned capons and rice—that was their dinner; and Captain Death spat out fishbones and took a whole capon and tore it with his dirty, hooked fingers, cramming his jaws and making a hoarse and gobbling noise.

Francis Farrington Sprigg ate like a cat, I swear, and daintily; and I even thought I saw his limber tongue travelling around his glass as though lapping the malt-brew foam.

Jack Ross ate not at all; but he drank enough, one elbow on the table; and ever his nervous fingers were in his disordered hair, or a-twitching and pulling at his hairless chin.

"That young lick-pot yonder, watching us from the dark till," lisped Francis Farrington Sprigg, "is he to be allowed to listen, Mr. Ross?"

"Freckles!" called Jack Ross. And, when I came to his side: "Do you mean to play the man? Yes or no?"

"Yes, sir—if you do."

"You cleave to me, then?"

"As close as may be, my—my friend and patron."

He shot a terrible glance at me, for I nearly had called him "my lord." Then the look of anger and fear faded in his reckless sea-gray eyes and he clapped me jovially on the shoulder.

"Here," says he to Captain Death, "is a young recruit for you, and we shall make a man of him yet if you sign him."

"And what will Tom Cocklyn say to that?" lisped Francis Farrington Sprigg, "if we crimp his young dish-licker out of his till and kitchen?"

"*Press*, not *crimp*," protested Jack Ross, laughing. "To press is to persuade—with kind words, and gently—"

Francis Farrington Sprigg wiped his prim lips with his napkin and looked around at me. Never had I seen such bland, cruel eyes or so long and sharp a nose.

"Where lies the station ship?" said he to me in his precise voice.

"Inside Cape Fear, sir, and off Old Clarendon."

"Do you ever go aboard Sir George Sayles?"

"Every two weeks, sir."

"With fresh fish, corn, and butcher's meat?"

"Yes, sir."

"In his frigate off of Topsail Inlet?"

"Yes, sir."

"The *Sea-Hawk* her name?"

"Yes, sir."

Francis Farrington Sprigg turned to Captain Death:

"How shall we know that this young rogue is not a spy?" he asked in his mincing, affected voice. And there was more cold terror in it for the slight lisp—like the faint hiss of a white-mouthed snake.

Captain Death's crummy voice was hoarse in my ears, now; and he began a-cursing and a-damning, and promising that Tom Cocklyn would strip the skin from my every bone for me if ever I turned false.

"Take him or leave him," broke in Jack Ross, disgusted. "Only you say you desire recruits for the *Black Bee* brigantine—"

"I did not ask for a litter of kittens!" growled Captain Death. "Send him aboard Sprigg and let them lap milk from the same saucer."

Sprigg's cold eyes turned on me. "Where is the *Sea-Hawk's* beat?" said he very softly.

"Between Cape Lookout and Cape Fear, sir."

"What signals does he set, off Topsail Inlet, to call Tom Cocklyn?"

"A reefed jack and a Dutch ensign at the main, by day; three red lamps at the fore besides her riding lights, sir—until answered."

"How does Tom call the *Sea-Hawk*?"

I lied and said I did not know. Said Sprigg in his lisping voice:

"What is that green light on the wood's edge yonder?"

"Where?"

"Where the pines end on the dunes."

There was a silence; then Sprigg got up out of his chair. Under the flap of his laced coat a heavy pistol sagged. He pulled it free, cocked it, and I thought he meant to blow my brains out.

Stiff with terror I stared back at him, but his calm, pale, murderous eyes were fixed upon Jack Ross, not on me.

"Have I seen you before?" he lisped.

"Have you?" asked Jack Ross, coolly.

"At Port Royal?"

"Possibly."

Sprigg's eyes never left Jack Ross, but he said to Captain Death:

"I told you so. We are come into a trap. This rake is youngest son to Lord Cardross, and a ruined man, who sells us this night to Sir George Sayles!"

"A lie," said Ross in a quiet voice; and lifted his glass and slowly emptied it. Then, looking up at Francis Farrington Sprigg: "I would not betray a guilty mouse that trusted me.... As for the rest—yes— I am John Ross. And I am ruined. And seek the sea to mend me."

"I told you so," lisped Sprigg to Captain Death. "Are we to be taken in a trap set for us by this penniless gamester and Tom Cocklyn—"

"Have done a-fiddling with your pistol!" said Ross contemptuously; but Captain Death shoved away the table and straddled to his feet.

"What do I care what his name may be?" he roared out in his

windy voice. "If he means to sign articles with me let him clap on his hat and come aboard me now!"

At that Ross turned, took his hat, shoulder-belt and sword from the peg where they hung, and, calmly smoothing out the plume, clapped the laced beaver upon his head.

"I am at your orders, Captain Death," said he gaily. But, even as he spoke, over his shoulder through the window I caught a glimpse of men moving like shadows under the cedar trees by the kitchen garden. And I knew that these three men were already doomed.

"Light us out," said Mr. Ross pleasantly.

So I took the candle to light them on their way to hell.

They followed me along the passageway to the barred door. Death, that was pronounced as it was spelled, awaited them outside. I led them lightly to their end.

By the dark back parlour Sprigg stopped, and, in his cold, fastidious, lisping voice, repeated his distrust of young Ross, of me, of Tom Cocklyn, and of The Lost Ship Tavern.

"All these smell of treachery a thousand leagues," said he, lifting his cocked pistol to fold his arms and rest it across his left wrist. It pointed at Mr. Ross.

"You murderous, milk-lapping leopard," growled Captain Death, "if you meddle with my recruits you'd best look to your rotting ship when I hail you."

Young Ross only laughed at Sprigg, careless of his horse-pistol and his pale, small eyes; and we moved on again toward the tavern door.

"Unbar it," growled Captain Death to Francis Farrington Sprigg. As he spoke, Jack Ross passed his arm around my body and drew me against him.

"Do you come with me, then, freckle-face—" he began in his careless, bantering way and suddenly became silent. His hand had touched my breast. The next instant he jerked me around to face him and saw the hot blush mounting from my throat to the roots of my yellow hair.

For a second our eyes met; then I dropped the candle and, at the same instant, Captain Death unbarred the door and flung it open, and strode out into the moonlight, followed by Francis Farrington Sprigg.

Before Jack Ross could stir I sprang ahead of him, slammed the door, and shot the great bolt of iron clanging through both staples.

"Bang!" went a musket outside, followed by a shattering shot from a horse-pistol. "Bang-bang!" went the muskets.

I heard a loud voice crying: "It's Captain Death of the *Black Bee!*— dead as bloater!"

Another shouted: "Sprigg's up again and running for the woods where the green lamp burns! After him, my bullies! Take him, my hearties! Tallyho! Stole away! Stole away!—"

I caught Mr. Ross by the sleeve and dragged him back through the parlour, through pantry and till and into the taproom.

He was deadly white but calm.

"You treacherous young wench," said he, "—so you've done our business for us, have you?"

"Not yours," I panted.

"What! Do you not mean to sell me to Sir George Sayles—you lying slut?"

"I sell nobody. I punish."

He glared at me in bitter contempt: "A tavern drab and a taker of blood money," said he. "Ply your trade, now, and end it!"

I came close and stood before him and spoke in a voice that trembled with passion:

"Say what you will of me, my lord, but I have promised God to help rid this world of the murderous gentry called pirates, who put my young mother to torture and outrage.... And left her dead; and my father tied alive to a hatch on his own deck.... And so set his ship afire in mid-ocean.... And so left them."

He stared at me.

"Nevertheless," said I, "I shall not deliver you up who have not yet signed their articles nor ever sailed On The Account. Follow me, if you please."

As he stirred not a finger I led him by the hand to the foot of the dark stairs, drew him up after me to the garret above, and so into my little chamber in the loft.

As he stood there, dumb, with shadowy, haggard gaze fixed on me, suddenly such a rage possessed me that I struck at him with clenched hands and gave him so violent a push that he stumbled backward and fell upon my trundle bed.

"You are more fool than knave," I cried in a choking voice, "or you should hang at Charles-Town between high tide and low—so hear me God!"

He raised himself on one elbow and lay looking at me out of his shadow-eyes like a damned man.

"Keep my chamber and stir not," said I, "until the *Sea-Hawk*'s men depart. Then get you back into Virginia where you ought to belong, and not in this Albemarle where live only mean whites and slaves and thieves!"

He thanked me very quietly. After a brief silence I heard men at the barred door below, and went down and opened. They were the *Sea-Hawk*'s men with their first mate, Mr. Wemyss.

He came in, closed the door, shutting out the crew, and, grinning, whispered to me:

"We shot old Captain Death to death, but Sprigg got away. Were there others?"

"None."

"My lads thought they saw three in the taproom—"

"I was the third."

"Oh.... Well, Sprigg had a longboat and crew inside the raceway. He's gone, damn him. His ship, *The Delight*, cannot be far off the inlet."

"God forgive you for letting him go, Mr. Wemyss," said I, trembling all over.

"I know," he said. "He took a Portuguese bark a month since and murdered all. He took a sloop belonging to Barbados, a Martinico man, and one, Hawkins, with logwood; and on the twenty-seventh, a Rhode Island sloop—and he tortured and murdered all.... Where is Tom Cocklyn?"

"Gone to Governor Eden in Edenton—he *says*."

Said the mate very solemnly; "Sir George Sayles bids you watch Tom Cocklyn for your life's sake."

"I have long believed that two masters pay Tom Cocklyn, and that he betrays both," said I wearily. "I am sick of men and their ways—sick to the bones.... Will your men drink a draught before they go?"

But he said he must get back to the *Sea-Hawk* with no more delay; and added that they were taking Captain Death along to hang him in chains on Execution Dock in Charles-Town.

When he went out I stood at the open door and watched the longboat's crew from the *Sea-Hawk* disappear into the night, lugging a corpse which was all bones and a bag o' guts.

After they had gone, I ran out along the dunes to the dead tree where hung my green lantern. With my crooked stick I unhooked it, lowered, extinguished it; and ran back to The Lost Ship.

In the kitchen was Moll Fair, too scared to speak; but black Herith sat asleep in the chimney seat. He had sailed On The Account in years gone by, and a shot or two from a musket was of scant interest to him—so that he fed fat and slept snug.

"A sailors' quarrel," said I to Moll. "Get you to bed."

She went, all a-shiver, whimpering at every step; and I at her heels; and shut her door tight after her. Then I went to my attic chamber where young Ross was lying as I had left him, resting on one elbow, his face in his hand.

"Come, sir," said I; "saddle your horse—for I do no more for you than I have done; and have no kindness in my heart for you; and so pray that I never see your face again as long as ever I shall live!"

He rose and followed me down the stairs, through the door, and out into the moonlit mews.

"Goodbye," he said in a gentle voice.

"God keep you from the gallows, my lord," I replied bluntly.

He stood silent for a moment. Then:

"What is your name, Freckles?" he asked.

"Nancy Topsfield, my lord. And if ever any murdering pirate learns it I shall know he had it from you!"

He gazed upon me in silence. God knows he was the handsomest young man I ever had beheld, and very beautiful in the moonlight.

Then, still silent, he took off his plumed hat to me and made me a most courtly bow.... The first bow ever offered to me by any man in all my life.

And so left me there in the swimming lustre of the Sea-Rogue's Moon.

CHAPTER II
CAPTAIN DEATH

Now it was in the dark of the Rogue's Moon, that month when affairs were brisk at The Lost Ship Tavern: gentlemen travelling overland from Charles-Town to Bath-Town, and even as far as Tyrrel Precinct.

Tom Cocklyn, my master, and host of The Lost Ship Tavern, served his guests with his own malt-brew and West Indian spirits in the taproom.

I was kept busy running hither and thither between till, kitchen, and stable, what with helping black Herith, the cook, to pluck capons, and Moll Fair, our tavern maid, to wash dishes; and also caring for the gentlemen's nags, to bed, rub, water and feed them; and avoid their teeth and heels.

Oh, yes, gentlemen all!—and they must have their muddy boots and spurs cleaned and their riding cloaks brushed; and one young dandy desired to have the plume curled on his gilt-edged hat— which I accomplished with a hot brad-awl.

And had a bit of Spanish silver of him; and he called me a likely lad.

Being a girl and no lad, I was ever in deadly fear of crooking my thin legs to bob a curtsey instead of touching my ragged hat or pulling a curly forelock for thanks due. But never yet had so revealed my sex, even to Tom Cocklyn.

The talk—as always in these times in North Carolina—was of piracy and pirates; for old Providence Island, or Skulltown, as some called it, was not so far off; and it swarmed with sea-rogues; and, year after year, they continued to sail the coast and the high seas despite Spanish Garda del Costa, and station-ships of the Royal Navy on guard, here and there all the way from Nova Scotia to where the Spanish Grants begin.

So, when travelling gentlemen, who gathered in taverns, discussed not rice, indigo, and tobacco, their talk usually was of pirates.

Now, one of our travellers was Nicholas Trott, Esqre, Chief Judge of North Carolina; and his visit frightened my rascal master, Tom Cocklyn. With the old Judge were two Assistant Judges, whose names I do not recollect. But were bound for Bath-Town where a Court of Admiralty was holden, and there to try some wretches taken in plain piracy near Currituck Inlet, who belonged to Captain John Rackham's crew, who had been mate in Vane's ship; and these were surprised inside the inlet ransacking a pink by Sir George Sayles's station-ship, the *Sea-Hawk*.

Tom Cocklyn, serving out Vernon grog to our guests, broke a tray of glasses—he having but a thumb and forefinger on his left hand and never would tell how he lost them—and bawled to me to come from the kitchen and sweep broken glass from the taproom. Which I did do presently.

As I was serving the gentlemen with flip, Judge Trott, a gaunt and owlish man with the pale eye of a starved hawk, shook his snuff-stained claw at Tom Cocklyn, and, says he:

"You may take my oath of office on't," says he, "they shot Captain Death through the body, and they took him by one of his spider legs and dragged him on his bloated belly to the water's edge. And when they shoved off their longboat and were come again for his dead body to hang it in chains, according to law, why, dammy, the dead body was up on its spider legs and went a-waddling and a-straddling away across the seaward dunes; and they never did catch him, what with the pine woods and a blood clot on the moon!"

He blew his snuffy beak, swallowed half a tumbler of grog, pulled at his long clay pipe, and looked palely at Tom Cocklyn.

"And that's the story Sir George Sayles tells in Charles-Town, Tom Cocklyn. What do you know about it?" he croaked.

Cocklyn said with an oath that he had been in Edenton on that night.

"Yonder lad," said he, "was alone here with black Herith and Moll. Tell the gentlemen what you know about it, Freckles."

I had both hands full of empty leather jacks, to fill them, but I paused on my way to the bar, and turned to face the several gentlemen at table.

"Sirs," said I, "Captain Death and Francis Farrington Sprigg had been drinking here, and when I let them out, Francis Farrington Sprigg went first, then Captain Death. Then—bang! went a musket!"

"And what next?" croaked Judge Trott.

"Why then, your worship, I pushed the bar through the door-staples and went very softly to bed." Several gentlemen laughed, and one said:

"You went very softly *under* the bed, I suppose, Freckles."

"Boy," said Judge Trott, "is that all you know about it?"

"Except what your worship is pleased to have told us."

"Hum-hum! Exactly. You—ah—say you were quite alone here, and Tom Cocklyn absent?"

"Mr. Cocklyn says so, sir."

Tom Cocklyn turned around in the till, and says he to me in a noisy voice:

"Was I in Edenton or was I not, you little swipe?"

"You *said* you were—"

"Damnation, was I *here* or was I absent?" he roared.

"Were you present but concealed, Mr. Cocklyn?" I asked innocently.

"That lad," remarked one of the Assistant Judges, "would make an excellent witness at law to hang anybody."

"He'd make a damned impudent witness," growled Tom Cocklyn. "Get away from here," he added, aiming a kick at me—which I avoided and shrank aside into the pantry, where I remained until the several guests began to demand their cloaks and boots; and then their horses.

So to the stables again, and there saddled their nags and fetched them around, five at a time, to the tavern door; and had a little money of my gentlemen for my pains as they mounted, one by one, and took the rutted road to Bath-Town.

When, finally, the last guest had drained a stirrup-cup and departed and the three magistrates in their sombre bellying cloaks had ridden away flapping like three huge and black-pinioned birds, Tom Cocklyn went out to sit on the settle under the tavern window where he could have his pipe and grog and spy-glass, and bathe him in the crimson rays of the declining sun.

He was a dirty man, seldom shaven, and wore a scratch-wig, a soiled red neck-cloth and a cocked beaver with grease spots on it, pulled low over one eye—the yellow one. The other eye was a pale bottle-green in hue.

Nights are chill at Topsail Inlet. I was splitting fat light-wood for the kitchen when Tom Cocklyn called to me:

"Come here, you spindle-legged, knock-kneed rogue!" And, when I came to him: "Do you want me to skin you alive? Hey?"

"No," said I, "I don't."

"Then mark me well, you yellow-headed rascal: when I say I'm away from home, *you* say so, too! Do you hear?"

"I don't wish to lie—"

"Lie! Why, you kitten-faced lick-pot, what d'ye mean? Was I here the night they shot Captain Death?"

"Yes, sir, you were."

"What! Do you pretend you saw me?"

"Yes, sir, I did—among Sir George Sayles's men."

"You're mad," he shouted at me; "what was I doing, then?"

"I don't want to tell you—"

"Answer!" he yelled in fury.

"You shot Captain Death through the body."

The silence frightened me; but I could not have replied otherwise, for my tongue is so oddly fashioned that it utters untruths with difficulty. And some day is like to undo me.

"Come here," said Tom Cocklyn.

He beat me very often, and kicked and cuffed me about; and it always hurt, for I was thin, and a girl —though he did not know that, nor did anybody else on earth excepting only one young man. And he in Virginia, I hoped.

So I went reluctantly and stood in front of Tom Cocklyn where he was squatted on his green-painted settle and a-sucking his long clay. There was ferocity in his face but he spoke quietly enough:

"You've come to learn too damned much," he said, "and you suspect more. Very well, here's the rest of it; I serve who pays me best—Sir George Sayles, Governor Eden, or gentlemen who sail On The Account.... Who bids highest wins me."

He gave me a terrifying look out of the greenish eye; the other, in shadow, shone dimly like an animal's eye in the dark.

"Now, you mewling little swipe," said he, "I'll strangle you with this"—he thrust his hairy, mutilated hand toward me—"and I'll chop you to pieces with that axe if ever you spit a word o' this to any living soul."

I was so frightened that I could scarce speak: "I shan't tell anybody," said I.

"That's better. Is your mind and your damned disposition firm in my service? Or would you snap at the kind hand that feeds you?"

I said: "If you shot Captain Death, I care not."

"Why, that's better still," said he. "All you have to do is to mind your own damnation business, and I'll attend to mine. And if ever you see me a-doing of queer things, just you take no notice, like a good boy, but go right on a-washing o' them pewter dishes. You understand me, Freckles?"

"Yes, sir."

"And when I tell you, go show a green light in the woods, it's none o' your cursed business why—is it?"

I shook my unkempt head.

"Or if you think you see me hereabout when I tell you I ain't here but I'm to Edenton—is that your hellish business?"

With the only finger on his left hand he poked the ashes in the bowl of his pipe:

"Moreover," said he, "if you think you seen me a-shooting of anybody whosomever, why, is that any o' *your* rogue's business?"

He took a pull at his grog, then at his pipe, then put up his spyglass and levelled it at the horizon.

"I'd just as soon skin you to the bones as skin an eel," he growled, squinting through the glass with his greenish eye. "And what's left

I'd bury in the hog-yard.... And if anyone asked, I'd say you'd run away.... Five guineas reward.... That's what I'd offer. On a printed notice.... Runaway indented servant.... Yellow-headed, freckle-faced, knock-kneed, skinny-legged lad. And a great liar.... Runned away from his kind, good master.... Meaning me.... And, all the time, the hogs a-rooting and a-gruffling over your bones! How d'ye like that? Hey?"

He continued to squint through his glass, and I continued to look at him. I knew he'd been a pirate. Doubtless a cruel one. Black Herith told me so. Said he'd sailed with him. Yet Sir George Sayles and Governor Eden paid him to inform on pirates.

And for this reason I never had attempted to run away. Because pirates had made me an orphan; and I had promised God to help rid the world of these cruel and wicked men.

The sun was nearly level with Tom Cocklyn's spy-glass, now, and how he could look into the red eye of it I do not know.

"A sail," said he, "hull-soused. Topsail schooner. Bound for Bath, I guess. Naval stores.... What the devil are you about? Carry that splinter-wood to the kitchen!"

The firelight in the dusky kitchen gleamed red on the gold hoops in black Herith's ears. He gave me a hot hoe-cake and a slice of bacon for my supper.

I carried it out to the barn, but the chickens kept jumping and flapping to seize it, so I ran out across the dunes and half a mile beyond the pine woods, and sat me down near the water which was at flood and stained blood red by the sinking sun.

Now, as I sat there all alone on the sands, eating my hoe-cake and bacon, and licking the crumbs from my rough, thin fingers, something—some subtle sense of another presence, caused me to peer around over my shoulder.

A man stood there, looking at me. The shock of it made me feel faint with fear.

"Freckles," he said.

At the sound of his voice I got up on trembling legs, still weak from fright. But I knew him. He was the Honourable John Ross of

Virginia, youngest son to my Lord Cardross of Port Royal.

"What are you doing here at Topsail Inlet?" said I. "Are you come a-pirating again?"

"I came to see Nancy Topsfield."

"Have a care what you say, sir," said I in a low voice and glancing fearfully about me. "If you discover what I am to Tom Cocklyn God only knows what treatment might be mine."

"Do you think I would serve you such a trick, who had saved my life—and honour?"

At that I looked at him very hard.

"Yes," he said, "I came here one night in April last, a ruined man, to meet Captain Death. And to sign his shameful articles and go aboard him to sail with him under a black flag or a bloody one, and take all nations."

He came nearer; smiled kindly at me. His was a strange smile that surprised with its candour. I had not before seen this young man smile.

"Freckles," said he, "they shot Captain Death, and, I think, Francis Farrington Sprigg. And would have taken or slain me, also, had you not saved me. And shamed me back to manhood."

"Then you are not come here a-pirating, sir?"

"I am aboard Sir George Sayles—"

"What!" I cried joyfully.

"—And command the *Moth*, sloop-tender to the *Sea-Hawk*.... To take no flag only if it be a black or a bloody one. Will you be friends with me now, Freckles?"

"Sir," said I faintly, "I praise God that I drew you in the door when the muskets fired upon Captain Death."

"For that reason," said he, "I come again to thank you, Freckles. And never again shall be tempted to so base a design as was mine that April night."

He took a purse from his pocket—a very lean one—and offered it to me.

"I have drawn a month's pay in advance," said he with his candid smile, "—not much—but, one day, please God, I shall reward you suitably—"

"If," said I, "I would not sell a known pirate for blood money, shall I take pay for kindness done a friend?"

"I wish it! Lord," says he, "you are in rags, poor child—"

"I will not have a groat of you if I must run naked!"

After a silence he took off his laced hat, lifted my hand in his, kissed it.

"Then—thank you," said he gravely. And put away his purse.

"You are welcome, sir," said I, laughing of a sudden—not knowing why I laughed at all.

"And one matter I must make clear for you," said I. "Captain Death shammed death—and presently got himself to the pine woods, and has never been retaken. And Francis Farrington Sprigg was neither wounded nor taken."

In the dull red light of sunset I saw him knit his brows.

"That's bad," said he.

"Have a care, sir, that neither of these fierce men ever take you."

He smiled: "My only care," said he, "is that I shall take them—" His smile faded; he said, bluntly: "What would they do to *you?*"

I shuddered: "How came you into Topsail Inlet, sir?" I asked.

"The *Moth* lies below—to the east of the wooded point, yonder. My shallop is beached below. I walked hither."

I said nothing. I began to feel confused. He seemed, all at once to me, so grand a man, tall and handsome, and so mighty a gentleman—who once had called himself Jack Ross, bent on the vilest purpose ever man might hatch and entertain. And now, suddenly, he had become as beautiful to me as a vision.

There was nothing more, however, than this which could concern him and me—nothing further to say. Besides, I would have liked to go back and consider these matters all alone in my attic chamber. But, as I turned toward the tavern, I felt my limp and calloused fingers taken into his hand; and I blushed violently; and, looking up, saw his eyes fixed on the sea as he walked beside me with my thin hand hot in his. Presently he looked down at me.

"Once more," said he, mischievously, "you shall draw me a jack of malt-brew, Freckles."

"Tom Cocklyn is at home," said I, "so have a care, my lord."

"What of it?"

"Nothing, sir.... Only he has never heard of Jack Ross from me."

"I understand.... Go you in advance, then; and in half an hour I shall drift in, as it were, on this flood tide out o' nowhere."

We walked on through the gathering dusk. I don't know why it was so, but, somehow, I did not wish Mr. Ross to come into the tavern, perhaps because I desired to be alone; for my heart was very full and somewhat violent, and my mind bewildered with all these things. Yet, perhaps, I feared something, too, for him, in this dark tavern where lately he had been in deadly peril.

Now, as the woods ended, we stopped. He retained my hand a little in starlit darkness, then released it; and I clapped wings to my heels and flew to outstrip the swarming thoughts that whirled like a fiery cloud o' bees to frighten me.

I had run nearly half a mile, and was climbing the dark dune through sweet-bay and sea-grape scrub, when I saw a green light at the water's edge near to where Tom Cocklyn's boats were beached.

This amazed me, for we set a green lantern at Topsail Inlet only to signal to Sir George Sayles in his station-ship, the *Sea-Hawk*. And why Tom Cocklyn had done this I could not guess.

So I ran down across the dunes toward the beach; and when I came very near to the green light I heard a man groaning; and then, in the green glow of the lantern, I saw a man's head—only his head, with both ears cut off—sticking out of the sand.

I stared at it in horror; and, as I stared, the head groaned; and I saw it was Tom Cocklyn's head, there on the beach, as though severed from his body.

Then, up out o' the shadow of a beached boat, rose two men and seized me by either arm.

I fought, twisted, writhed, kicked, bit—all in utter silence—but they began to run across the sands toward the tavern, dragging me between them. And, coming to the open door, pulled me inside, through the back parlour, hallway, and flung me headlong into the taproom which was ablaze with candles and noisy with shouting men.

I had fallen on both knees, but was on my feet as swift as a cat.

And found myself facing a man with spindle legs and a great, bloated belly, and the pallid, caved-in features of a skin-stretched skull.

The man was Captain Death.

"Why, damn my gizzard," says he in his hoarse and crummy voice, "here," says he, "is the starveling, girl-faced boy who betrayed me! Why, damn my lights and liver—"

Noisy voices were stilled; his sea-rogues in their soiled silks and gaudy sashes stuck thick with knives and pistols, came from the rifled till, from bar and pantry, to gather around me where I stood terrified.

Captain Death's voice became a hoarse and windy roar—for he had been shouting curses at me all the time

"You knock-kneed swipe! You mewling lick-spit!" he yelled. "You lit a green light for the *Sea-Hawk's* men to take me; and when they were come you let me out the door into a blaze of musketry!"

With that he pulled a brass horse-pistol out of his silken sash and laid it on the table and sat down, trembling all over, belly and limb, and showing me his crooked teeth.

"You treacherous young rogue," says he in such a rage he could scarce speak, "Tom Cocklyn, buried to the chin, and both ears cut off, waits for the mounting tide to send his soul to hell! But, dammy, that's too tedious to suit me before I make an end of you—"

With an oath he seized his pistol in ungovernable fury and fired at me; and the ball clipped a curl of yellow hair over my right ear.

Through the swimming, choking smoke, I saw him get to his legs and tug at his hanger to pull it from the scabbard; but his sea-wolves were yelling and pushing close around me, now, and clamoring to make sport with me before they slew me.

"Very well," he said hoarsely, "tie him to the tabletop, and fetch that big trapped rat in the cage-trap from the pantry! And fetch from the kitchen a small iron pot!"

Some of the men began to laugh, and seemed to know what was to be done to me.

Struggling helplessly I was carried to the table and roped flat to the top of it so that I could not stir a finger.

One of the men crowding around me put a small iron pot, upside down, on my stomach. Another showed me a great, bright-eyed rat in our cage-trap, which I myself had set in the pantry that very morning.

Then they lifted the iron pot a little, and let out the rat to scramble from the trap and hide under the pot on my belly.

"Fetch a pan o' hot coals from the kitchen fire!" roared Captain Death.

I had not uttered a sound and now my tongue froze stiff with horror as I felt the rat under the iron pot, running heavy over my belly and beginning to scratch at my skin.

"Dump the fire on top o' the pot!" cried a voice. "When the rat feels the heat he'll burrow into his bowels—"

Then I screamed. And, at the instant, such a crashing blast of musketry blazed through the open window that it stunned me for a moment. There came a trampling rush of cursing, bellowing men; the table overturned carrying me with it. And I fainted.

When I came again to my senses I lay deep in Tom Cocklyn's great chair, my hair and face all wetted with chilly water, and my fingers tight hold of Mr. Ross, clutching his strong hand with both of mine.

"Cheerily," said he, seeing my eyes open. "All is well with you, Freckles."

After a little while I whispered: "Yes, my lord."

Then I saw Tom Cocklyn, his head in a bloody bandage. He stood near his robbed till, drinking with some men-o'-war's men, and cursing and damning and voicing a ferocious joy that Captain Death and his sea-rogues, at last, lay dead or taken every one.

CHAPTER III
MARY READ

Tom Cocklyn, landlord of The Lost Ship Tavern, sat on the settle under the taproom window, nursing an inextinguishable rage.

Since Captain Death, the pirate, had cut off both ears and buried him to the neck in the sand to die by the mounting tide, Tom Cocklyn nursed his wrath against all sea-rogues, brooded, moped, lived only to do some of them an ill turn.

He saw enough of them, for these wolves of the ocean frequented his tavern at Topsail Inlet when driven to Carolina for wood or water or other provision.

Also they knew him for an old pirate; and some among them had him in their pay; yet he also was paid by our Governor of North Carolina, the Honourable Charles Eden, and by others, perhaps.

But his mutilated ears inflamed his mind even more than his body; and, since that dreadful evening, had changed his noisy brutality into a kind of silent ferocity which made of him a sullen, venomous, inert creature that squatted all day long on the settle to watch the sea.

Such customers as came to The Lost Ship I served, now. He would have none o' them, scarcely return a civil greeting, scarce speak to anybody.

Around his rough, bullet-shaped head he wore a red and yellow madras handkerchief, day and night, to conceal his cropped ears, for, being nearly bald, neither his hair, nor his whiskers which were as thin and dry and wiry as hair on a sick dog, could conceal his crippled features.

One day two of Vane's men, escaping, came ashore seeking the King's pardon; and Tom Cocklyn took them to Judge Nicholas Trott, and they were tried and hanged. And God knows what evidence Tom Cocklyn gave against them to so rob them of benefit of the proclamation which I, with my own hands, had nailed up in our taproom for all to read according to law.

We have, in Carolina, a thick and bloated kind of snake which is as deadly as it is sudden. And made me think of my landlord and master.

For, one day, I saw a man and a boy land at the inlet from a shallop, and shout to us to fetch a side o' butcher's meat to Calico Jack, who was John Rackham, the pirate, master of the *Kingston*, prize ship.

And I saw Tom Cocklyn take a butcher's cleaver and run toward them. I know not what frightened them or seemed to warn them of his purpose unless it was the way he ran, crouching and leaping like a panther.

But they became, suddenly, panic-struck, and ran toward the pine woods; and Tom Cocklyn ran after them. And came again to the tavern after half an hour, where, in the yard, I saw him washing blood from his arms and apron and from the butcher's cleaver which dripped red to the handle.

That night he took a spade and a lantern and was in the woods for three hours. I heard him come in where I lay shivering on my garret bed.

We had no guests that day. There was no sound, no movement in the tavern save buzzing and circling flight of flies. Black Herith sat dozing in the kitchen chimney corner where, on the white ashes, a single coal lay like a glowing eye.

Moll Fair slept on the pantry bench, like the slut she always was. I had washed her pewter dishes for her, fetched light-wood and water, trimmed candles, and cleaned crumbs.

Eggs I had fetched. I cooped two broody hens. I fed the sow.

Now, with time to myself, I took my school books to the back door and there seated myself upon the warm stone. Now, very earnestly, I fell to learning what I could out of these same books which I had as a gift of Mr. Ross of Sir George Sayles's company—who commanded his Majesty's station-ship, *Sea-Hawk*; and Mr. Ross commanded her tender the *Moth*, sloop, patrolling the North Carolina coast from Old Clarendon to Currituck Inlet.

After a while I heard Tom Cocklyn bawling: "Boy! Here!—you lazy rogue!"

Neither he nor Moll nor anybody ever had suspected my real sex, save only Mr. Ross who had surprised it.

I ran with my books through the tavern and out the front door; and saw Tom Cocklyn lumped upon the green settle in the sun.

"Here," he growled, "look through my spy-glass, for my good eye fails, what with the sun-glare and floating specks—"

One of his eyes was yellow; the good one was greenish gray.

I took the glass, levelled it.

"A tall ship," said I.

"Dammy," said he, "I can make her out, too. Does she carry colours? I can't see that very clearly."

"Not a shred."

"What do you make her, Freckles?"

"A large merchant out of England, inward bound—yet—how can that be, for she rides light—unless in light ballast—"

"Hell's roaring headwinds!" he growled, "does a tall ship arrive in the plantations in ballast? … Or some sea-rogue has taken and plundered her and put guns and crew aboard, or she's traded in the Indies and sails to Virginia for tobacco.... What's her bearing, now?"

"North-west by north."

"No colours?"

"No, not a rag."

"Guns?"

"If she triced up her ports I could tell you better. I see none—not even a swivel."

"What sail?" he grunted.

"All set, I think."

"What speed?"

"Scarce any.... None, sir, by her bow-teeth. Taken aback, now—"

"Teeth all pulled?"

"Clean. Her sails all shake. She gathers stern-way. I think she is in irons, sir—"

"Give me my glass— By God, she's in irons!" ... After a long silence: "She misses stays. What animal handles yonder helm? ... Now! They pay her off to starboard. Now they trim her. Starboard helm! So! She's under way again—on the larboard tack—"

As he spoke she passed from sight behind the pine woods.

"Who is the great fool who thinks he is sailing yonder ship, I wonder?" growled Cocklyn.... "And what is she? Out of her course? ... A tall ship, hey? A-sailing around Hatteras.... Yes.... Perhaps.... Calico Jack sails a tall ship, too.... Jack Rackham. With his light o' love, Bonnie Anne Bonny."

"Anne Bonny?" I repeated.

"The female pirate. There's five hundred guineas posted for her, dead or alive.... And the same for Mary Read, her ogre comrade. Mary Read; six feet o' bone and muscle and a man's beard on her chin! Yonder ship may be Rackham's. The *Kingston*. ... On a larboard tack, too. Yes, by God."

After a silence I said to him in a low voice: "What you did that day in the pine woods you and God only know.... But if it be truly John Rackham in yonder ship, perhaps he will anchor and send a boat to ask questions of you."

Then Tom Cocklyn began to damn and curse and grind his raging teeth and fling his spy-glass one way and his long clay pipe another. When he had done with his rage:

"Nevertheless," said I, "you had better consider what countenance to make him if he lands and comes here. Or else you had better take horse and go to Bath-Town or Eden-Town."

"Boy!" he roared, "d'ye think I'm afraid of Calico Jack?"

"You have no more ears to cut," said I, "but still have a throat."

At that he fell into such a fury that I drew away and stared at him as I might at a dog in a fit, and he a-swearing and a-damning me and John Rackham and every living creature that came into his furious mind.

That storm passed, too. He made me fetch his pistols. I picked the flints for him; loaded both and primed the pans with dry, bright powder. Then he shoved them into his belt and buttoned over them his dirty surtout.

"Freckles," says he, "you take your slate and chalk and your two books and run along the dunes and through the woods to the hill above Hangman's Point where the wrecker's beacon stands. And you can keep one eye on your book and t'other on yonder ship to spy out what may chance. And if aught happens to awake your distrust, you shall leg it back to me. You understand? Hull down, and you may take a nap if you choose. At anchor, you stand watchful guard. A boat, you lie flat in the beach-plums and observe. And if any men land and come this way, run swift as a dune-fox to carry news of it to me!"

I promised. I left him there on the settle, cursing, grumbling, and fondling his loaded pistols, his green eye glaring at the sea.

When, at length, I came to Hangman's Point and sat down on the hot sand among the beach-plums, I saw that the ship was nearly naked of canvas and lay at anchor above the wrecker's beacon.

There was no beacon, now; only a dead and twisted cedar with a horse's skull nailed to it—the skull of a blind, gray mare used by rogues for carrying a lantern to lure ships to the sands.

Nothing was happening aboard the anchored ship. I opened my book and read very slowly in it how to spell properly in our English language. Then, with slate and chalk and my other book, I set down figures to add, multiply, and subtract—always keeping one eye on the distant ship.

It was pleasant; for I loved hot sand and a good hot sun, perhaps because I was thin and young and not well nourished; and the man's work I did kept a girl's slight frame very meagrely covered.

Nestling there in my sand-nest among bayberry and beach-plum, where hundreds of big, wind-blown butterflies, yellow and orange, fluttered and drifted westward—arriving from heaven knows where and journeying I know not whither, I contrived to cipher, with chalk and slate, and still keep an eye on the ship.

Nothing stirred aboard her that I could see where she rode at anchor.

Sand, wind, and sun were hot, and the water of the inlet invited me. So presently I laid aside slate and book and, still keeping the seaward dune between me and anybody aboard the ship who might be observing the coast through a glass, I quickly took off my small-clothes, stockings and shirt and ran down to the water.

And there I lay and splashed in the cool delight of it—running up to the top of the dune to take a peep at the ship now and again—but noticed nothing extraordinary and returned to my crystalline bath.

Out into the deep bluish-purple current of the inlet I swam, and there sported and floated—how long I did not realize, until, suddenly remembering the ship, I swam to shallow.

There, rising and wading toward the sandy shore, I had nearly reached the beach when, to my amazement and fright, I saw a figure, suddenly dark against the sky, rise up above the dune and come over it and straight down to the shore.

The figure was that of a young woman, though clothed in a strange and wanton fashion. For she wore a scarlet silk vest, open to her belt, and very wide breeches of scarlet silk that fell only above her naked knees; and, around her hair—which was brown, and blew loosely about her face—was bound a gold and red figured handkerchief of Barbary tinsel stuff.

I stared at her in fear and astonishment—at her naked, sunburned body and her legs in sagging boots of soft gray leather, at her belt of shot silk which bristled with pistols and daggers, at the short, heavy, guardless sword which she carried in its silver filigree and crimson velvet sheath.

It was not until she had arrived nearly at the water's edge that she lifted her brilliant dark eyes and saw me. And plainly was as astounded as I.

Then, of a sudden, she began to laugh; and called out to me in a pleasing and merry voice:

"Well, then, what are you, little one? A sea-sprite?"

I knew not what to answer, and stood there ankle-deep in water until, smiling still, she bade me come ashore and fear nothing.

"For," says she, "you may take me for a female pirate, and you may be right, but I am a very gentle one to children and would do a harm to no living creature only if driven to it."

So I waded timidly ashore; and there knew not what to do, for I did not wish her to see me dress in my boy's garments, yet did not desire to remain naked.

"Well," says she, watching me with her frank smile, "if you mean to bathe again, sit here and clothe yourself with good hot sand while you tell me your name and your quality—for," says she, "you are a pretty child and daintily fashioned, body and head, hand and foot, but seem cruel thin in rib and limb."

So I made for myself a hollow and clothed myself in hot sand.

"What is your age," said she. "Fifteen—or less?"

"Seventeen."

"God have mercy—do they starve you then?"

I lowered my head and made no answer for a moment, then, looking up at her:

"Madam," said I, "are you Anne Bonny?"

At that she clapped her hands which were small, brown, and pretty, and burst out a-laughing.

"And where did you hear of Anne Bonny?" says she.

"Oh, madam, there are ballads and broadsides enough—"

"And printed bills of reward," she said. "You've seen and read them?"

"Yes, madam."

"Five hundred guineas, dead or alive? For Anne Bonny, the female pirate? Is that it?"

"Yes, madam."

"Come, then, and what further?—so you should know her and carry news of her to Nicholas Trott, and deliver her, and become rich, and marry a prince!"

"She sails with John Rackham in his tall ship, the *Kingston*, they say; and is his sweetheart."

"True. What else?"

"But—she is said to be no older than I, and small and light-haired, with very large blue eyes.... And I think you must be nearly twenty-one, madam, and are tall and brown."

"All that you say is very true, my child; and, as you see, I am not Anne Bonny. But am comrade to her; and Jack Rackham is my Captain, and the *Kingston* is my ship. Now, then, who am I?"

"Madam, I do not know."

"Why, then, I'll tell you; I am Mary Read.... What! You never heard o' me?"

"Yes, madam. But they say of you that you are six feet high and man-like and fierce of visage, with a sprout o' hair on nose and chin—"

Her uncontrolled laughter rang out in the silence, and so wildly she laughed that she pressed both pretty hands to her naked bosom and sat there rocking and gasping and the tears starring her dark eyes.

"Child," said she, "listen to me—for I shall sail again in two hours and never return; and it makes no odds to me that you know the truth and tell it—though nobody is like to believe you. Shall I reveal myself as I am?"

"If you please, madam."

"Well, then, give me your hand, there!—and look me well in the eyes—so! Do I seem very fierce and murderous?"

"No, madam."

"Cruel?"

"No—"

"Degraded? Debauched? Shameless?"

"Oh, no—"

"Have I bristles on my nose and chin—" She choked with laughing and laid a delicate finger on the tip of her beautiful nose.

"No," I said.

"Yet," said she, "I am that same Mary Read; and I am, as they say—a pirate; and very visibly a female."

After a while I asked her in a low, embarrassed voice, why she followed so violent and bloody a career who was young and handsome and in her early youth.

"My child," said she gaily, "I shall answer you the exact truth. My poor mother, to gain an annuity, promised by my grandmother to any grandson, passed me off for a boy. Always I wore boy's dress as a child. And ever after, too. When my mother and my grandmother were dead in London-Town, I thought a lonely boy had a better chance in the world than a girl. So I listed and served; and in the horse and in a foot regiment; and nobody ever suspected my sex. I desired to have a commission; but such are always bought and sold, and I had no money. So I went to sea as a fore-mast man; and, on the first voyage, the ship was taken by pirates, and I pressed by Calico Jack who was mate aboard Vane. I have sailed since with Jack Rackham, after he bade Vane go to hell and took the *Kingston*. And always was hoping to escape—until—"

She fell silent, and I saw a strange and tender look come into her brooding eyes.

"Child," said she, giving me an odd glance, "it is love that holds me aboard Jack Rackham.... Your unripe years tell me that you never yet have known that pretty passion.

"Yet, believe me when I tell you that Love, and her twin sister Hate, govern all the world."

Her brown eyes grew remote; she sat playing with my hand in silence for a while. Then caught my eye and smiled.

"A strange world, my pretty," said she. "Would you believe a young female could be a sea-rogue, and live among them, and still remain chaste?* Yet this is so.... Then, in April last, Jack Rackham chased the *Blue Dove*, galley; and coming up with her took her by the board off French Hispanola. And pressed the likeliest men aboard.... And among them a young man—pleasant, gentle, very honest.... Paul West, his name.... And Calico Jack gave him choice—or sign articles with him or die with others aboard the *Blue Dove*."

She took my hand and laid it on her heart: "Do you feel the beat, little one? That is love, ever babbling in my breast when I speak this young man's name.

---

* It was quite true of Mary Read.

"Do you wish to hear how well I love him? Well, then, last night my lover, Paul West, quarreled with Dick Corner, our quartermaster, who is a very bloody and powerful fellow; and Paul is peaceable and unskilled in arms.

"By our articles the law is this, that all such quarrels must be settled the following day ashore.

"Jack Rackham named the hour as five o'clock this afternoon.... What time is it now?"

She pulled from her silken vest a gold watch: "Two o'clock," said she gaily, "and in a little while you shall dress and hide yourself among yonder bayberry bushes; and you shall see a girl-pirate fight with Dick Corner for her lover's life!"

"M-madam," I faltered, "what are you saying to me!"

"What is true. For I knew this quartermaster bully would kill my lover. And I went to him in Jack Rackham's cabin, and struck him and cursed him and flung a can of rum in his face, and spat upon him. And I said to Jack Rackham, 'Three o'clock ashore tomorrow, or Paul West robs me of my pleasure!'

"'Dammy,' says Jack, a-roaring with laughter, 'if you have not frightened poor Dick to death you shall use him as you can at three o'clock, you pretty devil!'"

"Madam," said I, turning ill with astonishment and fear, "is it your present and instant purpose to bare that tender woman's body to this ruffian's sword and pistol?"

"To what purpose should I live if he killed my lover?" said she, calmly. "But now Dick Corner must first slay me."

I began to cry, silently, the hot tears running down both cheeks.

"Hush," said Mary Read; "there was no other way, my pretty." She put one strong, beautiful arm around me and drew me to her.

"Presently," said she, "you shall rise and creep up the dune and lie perdu among the shrubs." She kissed me, smilingly— "And there, my pretty, you shall witness to what lengths a chaste, pure love may go.... And if it end badly for me, well, I shall see my lover very soon again... God knows his heart and mine."

"Madam, does your lover know of this terrible adventure?"

"God forbid!" Presently she looked at her watch again, then sprang to her feet and drew me with her out o' my couch of sand.

"Come," says she playfully, with a gentle slap on the buttocks, "run to your hiding place, if you would see the sport, for I think their shallop is already on its way ashore."

So sudden and deep and tender a spell had this young woman already woven about my heart that my tears blinded me, and I could scarce find my way up the dune and discover my clothing and make out to dress me.

Shivering there under the bayberry bushes, flat on my belly, and now chilled, now hot, as though with a swamp fever, I lay and looked at Mary Read.

She paced the firm strand, up and down, with light, springy step, swinging her Barbary sword in its velvet and silver sheath, and humming aloud a song in a gay, contented voice. God give me such a courage as was this woman's, to whom the world had given so infamous a name.

It seemed to me a very long while before I saw her halt and turn her head very quickly toward the seaward dunes which lay piled like snow mounds between the ocean and the sound.

Over these dunes came a huge, hairy man, all alone. Yet there must have been a boat's crew below him on the sea-beach, because he turned and shouted back to his fellows who were invisible to me:

"She's here! I'll not keep you five minutes waiting!"

Now, this vast, hairy bulk of a man drew a pistol from his belt and cocked it, and began to run toward Mary Read, yelling foul names at her and cursing her at every stride, promising to do her business for her first, and then for her puny lover, and assuring her he'd rather do it than eat his dinner.

When he came nearer he presented his silver pistol and fired at her. Not hitting her he flung it on the sand, pulled another pistol, and ran toward her—a dreadful, monstrous sight in his green velvet, plumed hat, and naked feet; and a fathom of heavy gold chain dangling and tossing about his thick neck and huge and hairy chest.

The second time he fired upon her, Mary Read shot him, so that his hat with the red plumes fell from his head and a wash of bright blood bathed his left cheek and his bearded jaws.

Never had I heard such awful cursing as burst from the wounded man's distorted mouth. He pulled his hanger from his sash and leaped at her; and I saw her Barbary blade flash as it met his, cling to it, twist it, force it down, down, lower, ever lower, till, as he disengaged it, she slashed him twice like lightning, and he let out a roar that might have been heard at The Lost Ship.

Now he went at her in such a panic of blind and bloody fury that she gave ground and ran like a July fawn. But ever—when he stopped to slash the empty air, baffled and in check—instantly she turned upon him and bled him anew with her quivering, reddened point, so that he screamed at her in crazy rage.

I was on my knees in excitement and terror lest this fearsome, gore-splashed man catch her in his hands and tear her to fragments.

It may have been the salt and sand in some mortal wound he had got that suddenly set him death-howling where he stood, naked blade quivering in his fist.

Instantly she glided toward him. He saw her coming, light-footed, shod with velvet, and pause very close to him, near, smiling, motionless.

Then, with infinite effort, he struck at her face with wavering sword, inarticulate, dying on his feet; and Mary Read passed her Arab blade through his body, whipped it free and sabre-cut him across the neck so that his head, loosened by the severed muscles, flopped over upon his right shoulder. Down he came in a drenched heap of soiled silk and jewels and blood-wet velvet.

I saw his thick, hairy fingers move on the sand a little, squirm in a spasm as his lost soul passed. Then the air sighed and whistled from his collapsing lungs and the heap of flesh flattened and lay red and soaking under the midday sun.

Mary Read looked down upon him; lifted her head and her brilliant eyes to me; slowly held up her Barbary sword in the fierce white sunshine.

Then, in silence, she turned and moved leisurely across the sands toward the sea-dunes where, by their longboat, unseen men were awaiting her dead body.

I stood among the bayberries and watched her passing slowly out of my sight; and it seemed as though I could not endure that she pass so utterly out of my earthly life, so strangely and passionately tender the chord she had touched deep—deep in lonely and unmothered depths within me.

I gazed after her, dumb, with quivering lips, throat tightening under the unuttered cry.

The first woman ever who had touched me, looked upon me in kindness since my mother died of her martyrdom aboard my father's burning ship.

Now Mary Read had reached the crest of the seaward dunes and there stood poised an instant, scarlet, hardy, graceful against the burning sky.

A great sob wrenched my chest, tore from my throat the strangled cry of desolation.

It was too far; she never turned her head; and, in a moment, was gone, leaving my straining vision empty save of the vast solitude of sky and sand.

Suddenly the wild onset of grief overwhelmed me, frightened me, and I began to run toward the tavern. And as I ran I sobbed drearily and wept aloud, and my feverish voice calling upon my dead mother, sometimes, and sometimes upon Mary Read.

CHAPTER IV
DRUMS AND BLACK COLOURS

Now Tom Cocklyn, although landlord of The Lost Ship Tavern, no longer paid any attention to his proper duties, and ended by leaving it to me to serve guests, make purchases, and settle accounts and all reckonings.

For so profoundly, so fiercely smouldered his unquenched rage since the pirate, Captain Death, had cut off both his ears, that he could think of nothing except his hatred of all pirates, and his ferocious purpose to revenge himself on any of these sea-rogues who gave him opportunity.

All day long he sat on the old green settle under the taproom window a-spying out with his brass spy-glass what distant sails passed on the horizon, and ready to send word to Sir George Sayles in his station-ship, the *Sea-Hawk*, or to Mr. Ross in his guard-sloop, the *Moth*, tender, to chase and take any ship which seemed suspicious.

He was brutal to me; often threw an empty jack, or a bottle or even his clay pipe at me, and kicked or struck me very frequently so that often I had cuts and greenish bruises on my face and body; and once a painful burn between my shoulders where his lighted pipe hit me and spilled burning tobacco down my back.

I do not know whether he would have treated me so heartlessly had he known I was a girl and not the thin, freckled, starveling lad I seemed: for he never kicked Moll Fair, our slatternly maid, but only cursed her and abused her with his venomous tongue when angry.

At times I thought he really meant to kill me, such devil's malignity distorted his features when enraged.

One night, in particular, when he thought to have taken Francis Farrington Sprigg, the dandy of all sea-rogues, who anchored at sunset off of Topsail Inlet, and came with a wolfish crew to carouse at our tavern. For no sooner did Tom Cocklyn's seaward gaze discover the ensign flying aboard Sprigg—which was a black flag with a skeleton on it, and called by Sprigg the Jolly Roger—than he bade me saddle and ride like a damned soul to Cape Lookout where, he said, Mr. Ross should be cruising with the *Moth.*

God witness that I rode willingly, having promised my blessed Saviour to help destroy all pirates who so wickedly had used my mother and father and left me orphaned in the world.

So when I flogged my gasping horse up over the sea-dunes at Cape Lookout, and saw no riding lights inside, nor any trace of Mr. Ross, I made a beacon of drift, and laid pine boughs on it to make it burn redly.

And all that night I fed my fire and waited and prayed. Then, with dawn, I looked out over an empty sea; and so abandoned hope; and got on my nag and jogged back to slavery at Topsail Inlet.

Francis Farrington Sprigg and his sea-rogues had gone; and Tom Cocklyn was in such a rage with me that he fired a pistol at me when I came into the stable-yard, and ran after me with his butcher's cleaver which streamed with blood from a calf he had been vealing.

And I dared not venture near the tavern until, after candlelight, Tom Cocklyn was abed. Then black Herith heard me at the kitchen door and let me in, a-grinning, where I had a crust and a rind o' cheese, the first mouthful in forty hours.

Still, there have been worse masters to indentured servants sold into service for redemption. And I, a castaway child, had so sold myself, pretending to be a boy. And Tom Cocklyn bought me where I wandered, starving, on a Charles-Town dock, after the *Anguilla,* Indiaman, had picked me up a-riding of a charred spar near to our burning ship on which my mother and my father perished.

The morning after Tom Cocklyn fired his pistol at me he came from the shore into the taproom, wearing wet sea-boots, where, with a pail o' water and a mop, I had been washing the floor. And was now sanding it and making designs of rings and stars upon it with the white sea sand. Which he kicked at and spoiled.

I flinched and shrank aside expecting a blow, but he only growled at me and drew himself a morning draught. Then he went into the till and got upon the high stool, and there, grunting, cursing, and with labouring breath, he wrote a letter; and sanded and sealed it.

"Ross is off the inlet," said he to me, "in the *Moth*, and is bound for Edenton. Here is a letter I have writ to our Governor Eden; and you shall go aboard Ross and so to Edenton, and there deliver to the Governor this letter. D'ye understand?"

"Yes, sir."

"And when Ross sails again for Topsail Inlet, you return with him."

"Yes, sir."

"And what the Governor gives to you to fetch to me, you answer for with your life."

He glared at me as he handed me the letter. "You're but a dead whelp if you lose a farthing!" he said.

"Am I to fetch money to you from Governor Eden?" I asked in a fright.

"Aye." He stared at me under scowling brows out of his two strange eyes which were of different colours—the one yellow, t'other pale and greenish.

"You've been honest—I'll say that much," said he, "though you're too puny to pay for your keep, more like a scrawny girl than a stout, strong lad.... Well, then, get you aboard Mr. Ross. There's a shallop awaits you."

I had no preparations to make save only to draw a patched jacket over my ragged shirt and put on a pair o' shoes with pewter buckles—too big for me, and one o' them gaped and showed my scarred toes.

I had a gentleman's old beaver hat from which somebody had long ago stripped lace and feathers. This I pulled over my curly yellow head and ran down to the inlet where was a shallop and two men-o'-war's men to row me to the *Moth* which lay out a little way where was anchorage and good riding. We were soon alongside her.

When I climbed like a cat to her deck I heard the mate order her underway. Then he shouted to me to go to Mr. Ross in his cabin.

So I ran below where an armed sailor showed me the master's cabin; and I went in.

"Well, Freckles," said he, rising from the table and handing me to a chair, "I am contented to have you as supercargo. Are you, also, pleased?"

I felt my face heating and looked away from him, murmuring that I was happy to sail aboard him.

"Freckles," said he in that gently jesting, charming voice I never had forgot, "you are a very ragged—well, let us call you a boy—"

"Have a care, in heaven's name, my lord—"

"Nobody is listening. And, moreover, I am not anybody's 'lord.' Why do you call me that, Freckles?"

"I once told you why: you look like one of our great folk."

He laughed; then he got up, and, from a locker, took a new suit of gray wool—breeches, jerkin and a new shirt, a cravat of fine stuff with tiny laced edging, thread stockings of gray, and two pretty buckled shoon.

"Nancy Topsfield," said he in a smiling whisper, "if you must be a boy, then you shall be a proper one."

At that my face flamed and I lost my tongue and manners.

But he seemed to understand, for he merely smiled and laid the clothing upon the table, and bade me strip and dress again.

When he had gone away I locked the door, flung from me my rags and clothed me swiftly in these new ones. Then I ran to the door and looked out, and, seeing him in conversation, waited until he noticed me.

He came into the cabin pretending astonishment at my handsome appearance; and I laughed in my excitement and begged of him a comb.

So, before the little looking glass nailed to the cabin door, I combed and arranged my short yellow hair, and tied my cravat to my liking.

"Now," says he, "you are a pretty ambassador, and they must treat you with consideration in Governor Eden's kitchen, and not send you to sleep with the swineherds."

He invited me to sit, and took a chair beside me, and took one of my rough, scarred hands.

"Poor little hands," says he in that sweet voice of his. "Too young to toil so heavily.... Yet slim and prettily fashioned for all their roughness.... Where got you that bruise?"

"Which one, my lord?" said I innocently.

"Good God, have you others on your body?"

I laid my hand over the one on my cheek bone and remained silent, ashamed to tell him I had been ill used.

After a silence he said carelessly that he would have a word or two with Tom Cocklyn concerning me.

"My lord," said I, smiling, "you yourself once kicked me."

"What!" says he, reddening to his hair.

"What of it?" said I gaily, "you took me for a tap-boy—"

"Nancy," said he, holding my hands very tight, "you shall instantly stand up and kick me on the shins!"

At that I laughed so that he also began to laugh; and we were very merry there in the cabin until, being close together, he kissed me, and the shock of it was so deep and sudden that I sobered instantly and tore free of him and lay back on my chair staring at him in silence.

Mirth died as sunshine dies out in a room when a cloud passes. After a little he got up and went to the port and looked out.

"Are you hungry, Freckles?" said he without turning around.

"Yes, sir."

"You mess with the men forward," said he. "I dare not ask you here lest suspicion stir and it be discovered that you are not the boy you seem."

"I had not thought to break bread with you, my lord."

"Well, then, I had thought it."

He began to pace the floor, casting a moody look at me from time to time, then curtly bade me go forward and satisfy my hunger.

And so I left him.

I never suffer any illness from the sea. There was a fresh southwest wind, and we scudded before it. Green water came aboard us at times, drenching the gun-deck and the cannon; and the scuppers foamed.

Mr. Ross was on deck now, and he beckoned me aft where he stood near the tiller. And there I bided until sunset made of sky and water a gold and crimson fairyland. The red orb went down behind the bank of haze which was Pamlico, as we passed in Hatteras Inlet.

North of us the stormy Cape jutted, veiled in the white smoke of breakers whose eternal cannonade came dulled to our ears.

Over Albemarle was a moon on the water—ah, God, how lovely, and how sinister—for there, close under our larboard bow, lay a misty world of ghosts and spectres where lately the reddened hatchets of the Tuscaroras had dashed half a thousand souls into heaven or hell.

There, too, among those foggy inlets and dim dunes, so deathly white and still in the moon's ghastly lustre, lurked sea-wolves; and denned there. And, to myself, I whispered a prayer of thanks and gratitude that the foul lair of Captain Death knew him and his blood-smeared pack no longer; and that they were now with their fellow devils of the pit.

We sailed through the spectral moonlight over Albemarle. While Mr. Ross had the tiller he neither noticed nor spoke to me where I sat huddling my knees under the after swivel.

But, when our quartermaster, Mr. Drere, took the tiller, he came and leaned on the stern-chaser, gazing in silence at the wake flowing from us like tarnished snow. And, after a while, I ventured to rise and lean there beside him on the long gun.

"Freckles," said he under his breath, "what countenance to his saving angel should a man make—who once was all but damned?"

I did not know bow to answer this young man who had been the first man ever to speak to me with kindness since my father died and his crew perished under dagger, shot and sword.

"If," said he, "I had money, I would buy you of Tom Cocklyn."

"To what purpose, sir?"

"To no ill one. Did you think that, Freckles?"

"No, sir. But to buy my indenture of Tom Cocklyn—why?"

But he only shook his head, saying, "The money I've wasted! God pardon me."

After a moment—for he looked very sad—I ventured to touch his arm.

"You are kinder to me than ever any living man has been. I scarce know why.... And ask nothing of you—"

"You are ill found at The Lost Ship, Freckles."

"I am well enough—"

But he shook his beautiful young head: "Had I a household—and a house to house it"—he laughed drearily—"and if I had money, too, why, I would place you in it and pay Cocklyn for his pound of flesh—"

"There are one hundred and six pounds, sir, including my bones."

We laughed together. Then he, swiftly savage and impatient:

"Damnation," says he, "I should have money enough to buy you if only I might lay a rich sea-rogue aboard! ... I should have four shares, Freckles, if the Court of Admiralty adjudged the ship to me."

What he said stirred me deeply, but to no happiness; because, for the first time, a fear concerning this man began to creep into my mind and slowly possess me. And yet, to risk death was his trade; and I had known it; and the thought had not consciously disturbed me until now.

"Well," said he, "take heart, Freckles, for I shall comb this coast till I discover means to free you of The Lost Ship."

With what he had said troubling my mind, I replied very innocently:

"I had rather do with Tom Cocklyn all my life than that you should come to a harm through any care concerning me."

"Why?" says he, laughing; and I felt his firm hand closing over mine.

"Because, sir, the world would be very dreary to live in—lacking you." Suddenly tears filled my eyes—I don't know why.

"Lord," said he, "what tender souls dwell sometimes in young and humble bodies!" Then he placed his lips to my ear and whispered: "Until I redeem you, Nancy Topsfield, how can I redeem the rogue I was?"

"My God, sir," said I looking around at him in the foggy moonlight, and the tears hot on my cheeks, "I tell you again and again I ask no pay for kindness done, and you are ever seeking to reckon with me. Sir, you anger me; and if ever I swore at all I would swear now and say damnation!"

I was so hotly aroused that I was astonished when he laughed.

"Very well," said he, "the little daughter of Captain Topsfield shall continue to hold the son of Lord Cardross in her debt."

"You owe me nothing!"

"I know what I owe you, Nancy Topsfield.... And here's one item on account."

His lips rested lightly as a moonbeam on my tear-stained cheek— an instant—

"Good friends," said he; "say it, Freckles!"

"Yes—good friends, sir."

"Go below," said he, "there is a bunk for you in the flag-locker."

So I bade him good night, still confused and a-quiver with emotions vague and unfamiliar; and nearly crooked my thin legs in a curtsey but bethought myself in time; and so turned and ran below to the flag-locker, and there lay in privacy and happy content.

I awoke in a fright and sat up naked in my bunk, and pulled the blanket up to my throat, for Mr. Ross stood by me saying:

"We must have our flags and instantly. Dress swiftly, Freckles, for I think we have a sea-rogue under our larboard bow."

He took some folded flags from the locker and passed them to somebody outside, then with a gay and mischievous glance at me he went away in a hurry.

My clothes I seized and flew into. As I ran out I noticed buckets of water near the magazine, and, not heeding the armed sailor on guard, doused my face and hands in one, and so, still wet, hastened on deck where the sun nearly blinded me.

We were carrying full sail in a spanking wind; spume flew over us; gun crews were casting loose their guns, pulling out tomkins, moving hither and thither with swab and rammer and burning matches.

Mr. Drere had the tiller; Mr. Ross stood with levelled glass abaft the mast. High on the shrouds above a sailor clung looking out to the westward; and a lookout overhead was gazing, too.

Powder-lads ran to and fro between gun-deck and magazine; men appeared who served out cutlasses, pikes, and muskets.

I looked at Mr. Ross, but he did not notice me, so I made my way forward to the long gun in the bows. And from there saw a brig, under full sail, and so near that I was startled.

She was a dirty-looking craft with patched canvas, battered, rusty, and sailed with a foul keel and seemed deep-laden.

She had been painted green and white, but I saw no ports, no guns aboard her, nobody stirring, no flag.

Now, from the after deck I heard Mr. Ross shouting orders in his clear, powerful voice which seemed calm yet charged with gaiety.

I saw the gun-crew of the bow-chaser looking aloft; and I looked up and saw the Cross of St. George break out overhead.

Bang! went a swivel aboard us to confirm our ensign.

Then all eyes turned to the labouring brig; but she drove heavily on, showing no colours, taking no notice.

Then we dropped our ports and ran out our guns; and, under my feet, the deck jumped with the explosion of a heavy gun from our larboard battery. I could see the spray tower and spout up where the round-shot went a-skimming across the strange ship's bows.

Now I saw Mr. Ross climb into the shrouds to hail the brig.

"Ahoy!" he shouted. "Will you show your colours?" And, as nothing stirred aboard her: "Will you answer?" he cried, "or will you take a shot amidships? For, by the living God," cries he, "you look like a pirate and behave like a fool; so, for the last time, ahoy! and what damned ship are you and from whence do you hail!"

Then a shocking thing occurred; for, suddenly, the dumb stranger dropped her ports and her dirty sides yawned with guns.

At the same moment, upon her quarter-deck, men swarmed; a mighty roll of drums broke out aboard her and came loudly to us across the sparkling water.

Now, before my frightened eyes, a sombre flag crawled aloft, its dark, heavy folds unrolling slowly from her masthead; and there stirred and flapped. It was a black flag and it bore a human skull.

"Drums and black colours!" bawled our first mate. "Let her have it, my bullies, and be damned to her!"

"Down with your helm!" shouted Mr. Ross, "all guns for a broadside! Fire!"

The terrific out-crash staggered me; I clung to the rail in the stifle of swirling smoke. Through it a red flame lashed out at us from the pirate's broadside, and an iron storm swept through our sails and rigging.

Buried in smoke we then tacked; the pirate dropping astern; and we bore away before the wind, clapping on every rag o' sail we could bend. The pirate did the same, floundering to leeward, for she was as deep-laden as she could swim, and it was plain we had caught her with her shark's belly full.

When again we came within gunshot we had shifted our after guns, and now we raked her poop and cabin. Then came alongside and gave her the guts of our smoking guns, and took her broadside to lay her aboard; but could not come to it, so mangled and torn and splintered were we, already afire in two places, and our sails very badly riddled.

A shot struck our mast, shivered the hounds which fell and broke the bitts off. Another shot smashed the hatchway, starting planks under the gunwales and dismounting a port swivel.

So distracted was I in the swimming smoke and the shocking detonation of the broadsides that I staggered and groped about like one blinded, slipping up and down on the heaving and bloody deck where dead men rolled and wounded crawled away from the crashing guns.

Near to a dead young man who lay in the scuppers, I saw a pistol and a cutlass, and, taking the pistol, cocked and aimed it and fired upon the pirate ship as we hedged upon her once more to take her by the board.

Mr. Ross, hatless and coatless, his shirt sleeves rolled and a heavy hanger in his hand, stood coolly directing the helmsman while the brig's forward guns were being shifted aft where we had been a-raking her.

Now, alongside of the rover, we let go our great main-sail so that the long spar swung athwart the pirate's main-mast, carrying away stay and ratlin, and became locked with spar and rigging.

So deeply swam the pirate that from our larboard rail our bullies leaped downward onto the brig's deck, which was a welter of blood, top-hamper, and splinters.

Now when I saw Mr. Ross run out over our locked boom and spring upon the brig's quarter-deck, I ran after him as nimbly as a cat on a tree limb; and, seeing a great, naked, hairy fellow striking at Mr. Ross from behind with a pike, I gave him so hearty a cut with my hanger that he screamed out "Jesus!" and his pike fell from his fist; and a man-o'-war's man near me shot his head to fragments with a musket.

Our men had gone over with a cheer. They were still cheering as they boarded the brig, but never have I heard so horrid an uproar as the sea-rogues made, cursing, damning, and screaming like crazed women as our rush crowded them forward.

Suddenly in the smoke and flame and hellish tumult I saw their captain with his brawny, naked back against the main-mast and his little eyes glittering at me.

Instantly I knew him; and so great a horror overwhelmed me that I near lost my senses with the shock of it. For he was Benjamin Hornygold's brother, Israel, who had been quartermaster aboard Low; and he had murdered my father and my mother and burned them, dead or yet alive—I know not—in my father's great ship the *Fancy Nancy*.

He had but just slain one of our bullies with an axe when my eyes caught and engaged his. I do not think he knew and remembered me, but saw only my feeble youth and the stark horror blanching my features.

Instantly his whole visage writhed at me and he opened his awful mouth like a huge snake at me, showing two fangs in dreadful silence.

So stunned, so nerveless was I that he could have made but a step and sheered my head from my body with his broad-axe which was still red and dripping.

As he gripped the weapon with both hands to swing it, Mr. Drere came running on the other side and caught the broad-axe and struck Hornygold with a pike, tearing open the flesh of his neck.

With that the huge sea-wolf let out a howl and slashed at Mr. Drere, but missed him and drove his axe deep into the mast.

Then blind fury seized me and I ran to him and took my heavy cutlass with both hands and gave him a stroke which cut through his left arm so that it broke the bone and swung and dangled in its gore.

Oh, God, what a yell, which seemed to tear through his lungs and throat and scatter a foam before it.

And, still yelling like a damned man, with his huge right hand he tore the broad-axe blade from where it stuck in the mast and swung it to cut my body from my legs. And at that instant Mr. Ross ran up and shot him in the belly with a great horse-pistol.

So terrible the blow of the swinging axe that, missing me by a hairbreadth, it severed the halliards and nearly sheered away the mast again.

Then I drove my sword into him; and Israel Hornygold, the blood spouting out from his belly, dragged a silver pistol from his sash to slay me. But, as he cocked it, the great black flag with its death's-head, fell from the severed halliards and enveloped him; and, as the agonizing and dying wretch floundered in its sombre folds which blinded and stifled him, his pistol exploded and set the dark ensign afire. And our men ran in with pike, axe, and musket-butt and beat him to a pulp under the black folds of the flag: and I did not dream that any other save only a devil out of hell could be so mutilated and still stir and shudder and quiver, as does a snake though crushed to fragments.

Now, through the noises of exploding muskets and grenades, I heard the pirates bawling to one another that Israel Hornygold had struck; and, to us they yelled from cabin and forecastle, shouting up at us from below decks and calling upon us to give them good quarters.

Suddenly their drums sounded; and three half-naked rogues in gaudy finery marched out upon the quarter-deck and beat a parley with all the impudence in the world.

But I had turned sick with it all, and was too weak and ill to notice what was being done and what I was about, only that I lay for a time against the gunwales and close to swooning.

Then Mr. Ross's voice was in my ears, and I opened my sickened eyes; and he bent over and took me up in his arms.

I heard him tell Mr. Drere to take command of *The Happy Parrot*, prize, and choose six fore-mast men, and carry her into Bath-Town anchorage, following him in the *Moth*.

Then, I lying in his arms, he stepped from the prize to his own sloop and carried me below and laid me on the bunk in his own cabin.

There, looking down upon me: "Are you hurt?" said he.

"No, sir. Sick and frightened."

He began to laugh: "Frightened! Why, you fought like a wildcat, Nancy Topsfield! Do you not know that it was Israel Hornygold you fell upon with your little cutlass and frail arm!"

Feeling faint again I closed my eyes:

"It was he," I whispered, "who took the *Fancy Nancy* by the board, and murdered my mother and my father and burned them in my father's ship."

After a long silence, lying with eyes closed, I heard Mr. Ross's grave voice:

"Hornygold is in hell: and you shall think no more of far-off sorrows and the grief of days that God alone shall mend."

"I am very weary, sir," I said, "and would be well dead."

"Would you hasten God's purpose, Nancy Topsfield?"

"No, sir. But—I am very lonely.... I think I am the loneliest among all on earth."

There was another silence; broken by the sound of hurried feet on the companion, and Mr. Drere's voice loud in excitement:

"Lieutenant Ross! Best news for you of *The Happy Parrot* prize!"

"What is it, Mr. Drere?"

"Sir, her hold is crammed with African and Spanish plunder—silks in bales, madras, East India silver and spices, gums out of Africa and ivory; and bar silver piled like Holland bricks—"

"Very well, Mr. Drere. Go aboard, sir. I follow to set your course."

Then, seeing me staring at him with wide eyes, he began to laugh; and, laughing, leaned over and kissed my tangled yellow hair.

And so left me to lie and wonder and remember. And sometimes close my eyes to think on him.

CHAPTER V
THE GARDEN OF EDEN

I knocked. A servant in yellow livery, turned up with purple, opened the door a little way. When he beheld what he supposed was a boy carrying a sealed letter, he offered to take it out of my fingers. But I told him politely that I was pledged to deliver it to Governor Eden into his proper hands; and, after a sharp dispute, he let me in and left me standing alone in an elegant hall full of fine pictures in golden frames and beautiful polished tables and chairs of walnut with very slender spiral legs.

When he came again he bade me follow him, and led me through the hall to the rear where pillars framed a view of a most lovely garden. O heavenly angels! What a fountain of clear water was a-playing there amid such flowers as I had glimpsed only in Charles-Town where I once wandered a motherless, fatherless girl and a starving castaway.

I heard the servant say to somebody: "If it please his Excellency, here is the boy from Topsail Inlet with a sealed letter for the Governor of North Carolina."

Then I saw a pale gentleman with haggard, handsome features, seated at breakfast by a table beneath a huge live-oak tree.

He wore a laced coat of thin gray silk, breeches and stockings of the same, with a waistcoat of ivory satin delicately embroidered in pink rosebuds. And clasped across the filmy blond lace at his collar was a pin set with a great jewel that took the sun like a giant dewdrop.

"Well, boy?" he inquired gently.

"Sir," said I, "are you the Honourable Charles Eden, Governor of North Carolina?"

"Yes," said he with a faint smile.

So I bowed and offered my letter from Tom Cocklyn; and he broke the seal and read it, bringing it up very close to his wornout, handsome eyes.

As he read, tracing the scrawled lines with thin forefinger, the little colour in his face was fading to a pallor.

When he had read Tom Cocklyn's letter again he folded it and placed it in his pocket. After a moment he stirred the bowl of chocolate with a spoon and lifted his haunted eyes to mine.

"You lodge at the Eden Arms," he said pleasantly.

"Yes, your Excellency."

"Lieutenant Ross waited upon me last evening after putting you to bed," said he, smiling.

I blushed hotly: "Did he say that, sir?"

The Governor laughed in his gentle way: "You are too tall a lad to be put to bed by anybody," said he. "Well, no; he said that you had behaved very gallantly aboard the *Moth* when she was locked with the pirate Israel Hornygold.... I think you are a young, frail lad to show such determination and courage in action."

I did not know what to say, and stood restless and abashed upon the soft carpet of English grass.

Said he: "Mr. Ross tells me that your father was Captain Topsfield of the *Fancy Nancy*."

"Yes, sir."

"A sad affair," says he kindly, "—and Israel Hornygold murdered your parents and burned them in the *Fancy Nancy*."

"Yes, sir."

"And what became of you?" he asked.

"Hornygold's mate, Dick Greensnarl, noticing there were sharks about us, lashed me to a spar and towed me astern for sport."

"My God!"

"I got my legs free and then my arms; and I gnawed through the tow-rope.... They fired muskets at me until I had drifted out o' shot behind their wake.... And so, toward sunset, was discovered afloat by a ship and carried into Charles-Town.... And there, being destitute and very hungry, sold myself for redemption to Tom Cocklyn. And am indented servant to him in his taproom at Topsail Inlet."

"He uses you cruelly?"

"Not very gently, sir."

"You do not love Tom Cocklyn?"

"No, sir."

"Then—would you lay information against him?"

I reddened at that: "No, sir."

"Why not?"

I shook my head and said that I could not do that merely because he sometimes abused me.

"Yet you are secret and active against any sea-rogue," insisted the Governor, watching me.

"That is not private vengeance alone, sir, but in behalf of all innocent folk who live in dread of these wicked men."

He considered me out of his weary eyes, then the kind smile lighted them, and he bade me seat myself upon a settle where lay his spectacles and an open book.

When I had done so, he made me eat, filling a bowl with chocolate and bidding me satisfy my hunger: "For," says he, "all boys are always hungry, and I make no exception of so slim and pretty a lad as you who have behaved so well in combat."

So I ate bread with golden butter on it and spread it with honey, too. And there was a salad of palm tops, and cold fowl, and a dish of sugared cakes and another of white mulberries—which Mr. Eden told me to drench with cream.

O holy angels, never had I so banqueted in all my life before, and ate until I could not hold another mouthful.

"What is your name?" said his Excellency, looking up at me through his spectacles, and closing the book he had been reading.

"I have taken my father's name, sir, which was Annan Topsfield."

"Annan," he repeated. "Am I to call you Nan?"

That startled me, but I saw he had no suspicion of my true name and sex.

"Usually," said I, "people call me Freckles."

"That will do very well," said he, smiling. "So, Freckles, I shall send you back to Tom Cocklyn with a small leather bag in which is tied several pieces of minted Spanish gold worth a hundred pounds. And, with this, I send to Tom Cocklyn a letter, saying that I desire to purchase of him your articles of indenture and take you for my servant and page.... Does it suit you, Freckles?"

I could scarcely speak and was terrified lest tears betray my sex and weakness.

"Yes, sir," I gulped. "I would serve your Excellency very faithfully—and die very happily in your service—" I could not go on, so turned my head to look across the garden which seemed to swim like a tinted dream through my tears.

"Well," said he, "go you and stroll about the lawn under the pleasant trees, and presently I shall think what I am to write to Tom Cocklyn, and compose a letter for you to carry to him when again Mr. Ross sails into Edenton anchorage."

"Has Mr. Ross sailed, sir?"

"In company of Mr. Rhett in his sloop to take Charles Vane, the pirate, who is said to have passed in the Virginia Capes."

"Another sea-battle!" I faltered, thinking of Mr. Ross.

But the Governor did not understand my concern, for he smiled and said: "Hornygold's ship, *The Happy Parrot*, should make of Mr. Ross a wealthy man, and enrich all his crew when the Court of Admiralty sits. And if Mr. Ross and Mr. Rhett take Charles Vane, they may find him as rich as Hornygold.... Now go and wander where you will, Freckles; your bed and board are paid for at the Eden Arms Tavern until such time as Mr. Ross returns."

So I made him a bow and then drew on my new beaver hat, and walked for a while among the flowers. By hedges of oleander and pink and white and crimson hibiscus I passed, watching many little birds flying about the silver mosses trailing from the great oaks; and saw jewelled hummingbirds darting from bloom to bloom, and green and golden lizards panting on the garden wall.

Not for years had I roamed in so fair and sweet a land which was so unlike our sands and woods and sounds and salty barrens at Topsail Inlet where bayberry and harsh grasses grew, and the endless forest of high black pines walled us in to the ocean's edge.

I went out the garden gate and walked about the town of Edenton—a pretty place of some seventy houses or less and no church, but ordinaries a-plenty by the river. Everywhere tall glossy magnolia trees and oaks and sweet-gums, and the scented air heavy with jasmine, white and golden. Everywhere birds—mockers singing loudly, and wrens, and blackbirds with crimson epaulettes chattering among the river-reeds.

Few folk abroad; many blacks hauling tobacco and naval stores; and a lad fishing on a wharf where was a gallows, and a corpse hanging there a-sun-drying in irons.

I ventured to ask a woman who it was.

"Oh," says she, "yonder hangs Captain Blue-jaws who once was mate aboard John Quelch, and has dangled and sun-dried there these ten years. And, praise God," says she, "we are like to hang a row of wretches there this very day to keep him company; and others we shall hang a month hence when Judge Trott tries these rogues taken from *The Happy Parrot.*"

"Have you pirates in jail here?" I inquired.

"Six, and all condemned. Judge Trott departed yesterday; and six of Jack Rackham's rogues are to hang. You shall see a rare sight, my lad, twixt high water and low this pleasant afternoon."

I shuddered and went on along Fish Street and then by Charles Street and Princess Lane. Beyond lay Carteret Road, and I could see the jail there near the woods. So then to the Eden Arms, by Rosebud Lane, where it stands pleasantly above the river with water-stairs and a fleet of shallops, pinnaces, and dories below.

In the tavern taproom there was not a soul save the boy asleep behind the till spindles, and a puny youth sprawling by the window, his death-white visage framed in both hands, and staring up at the sky like a lost soul in the pit gazing out toward God.

I know not whether it was that my heart was very sore and lonely because Mr. Ross had gone again into battle that this sickly young fellow's white and tragic face stirred me to curiosity and pity.

As was customary, I bade him good day when I came in; and he started and looked at me with so hopeless a gaze that I walked to where he sat and asked him kindly if he were ill.

"Ill at ease," he said.

"I am sorry, sir."

But he covered his face with both hands and remained silent.

Twice I spoke to him, gently; and my voice is somewhat soft and girlish, and I think the tone of it stirred his desperate and overwrought senses to the breaking, for he lifted his tear-marred features in a panting, pitiful manner:

"Oh, God," says he in a dreadful whisper, "I cannot bear it longer and be dumb and silent and with no pitying soul to listen.... Boy— such sorrow is mine such terror—and God abandons me—"

A sob shook his bony frame. I took his trembling hand and covered it with both of mine.

"Sir," said I, "you may speak fearlessly to me who never have betrayed any creature that trusted me, and have, this day, a sad and sore and very suffering heart of my own."

"Are you also unhappy?" he asked, lifting his head from his arms.

"Deeply."

"Why?"

"Because," said I, "the only being on earth whom I dearly love is in danger of death at sea."

"Boy," said he hoarsely, "you seem tender and merciful, and I must speak—I *must!*—this loneliness and silence is slaying me with each choking breath I draw—"

"Can I help, sir?"

"Oh, God, no.... No! ... Only—"

I waited.

"Boy," said he, "they hang six of Jack Rackham's company an hour before sundown.... Do you swear secrecy?"

"God hears me swear it."

"Then—*I* was of that company!"

"You! A pirate!"

"No; and never was. And thus it befell me, and the others: A month ago Jack Rackham, flying a bloody jack and a black ensign, took a sloop off Ocracoke. Then he put me and six others of his company into the pinnace prize and sent us ashore inside Hatteras for to fill our water casks.

"Boy, I had been pressed aboard Rackham, and for three years awaited opportunity to escape.

"So when we were to arrive inside Hatteras at the springs by The Cedars on the main, I and a comrade planned to escape.

"But it was not to be, because Mr. Rhett in his sloop saw us, and chased us, and took all in the pinnace excepting me who had gone into the woods to look for the springs.

"And today," says he, wildly, "all six are to hang. And among them my comrade who is guiltless and was pressed as I was, and is dearer to me than life—"

He made a desperate gesture and got up out of his chair, but I pulled him back with all my strength, whispering that he should have a care lest the sleeping lad behind the till notice him and listen and inform against him.

"What is your name then," said I, "who sail aboard Calico Jack and are no willing rogue?"

He gave me a look, then: "I am carpenter aboard Captain Rackham—and my name is Paul West."

"Paul West?" said I, "where have I heard that name.... Where— from whose lips—"

Suddenly I knew that Mary Read who was called the Female Pirate had told me of her lover. And this was that same man!

"Paul," said I in a frightened voice, "answer me on your life and truthfully before God. Is Mary Read among those taken?"

"Yes."

"You mean—you mean that my pretty Mary Read is to *hang!*" I whispered.

"God pity us," he breathed, "she was found guilty with the rest and must hang with the others this day betwixt high tide and low on Eden sands—"

As he spoke there was a noise in the entry and there came into the taproom a heavy, red-faced, vulgar fellow wearing a very dirty neck-cloth and dangling some keys on an iron ring.

"Noah Gullet, the Provost Marshal," whispered poor West.

The Marshal went to the till and awoke the boy.

"Matt Sallam, our clerk, is taken with the fever," said he, "and I desire to have my bill made out if there is anybody in this tavern who knows how to write and figure with an inked pen."

The tap-boy knew of nobody. The Marshal turned and looked at Paul West and at me:

"If you can write my bill for me," says he, "there's a shilling for you, young man. Can either of you write and cipher?"

"I can," said I.

So he bade the tap-boy fetch ink, sand, and paper, and mend a pen for me. Then he went to the door and called out: "Come in, Jack Ketch!"

There came, then, out of the dark entry, a little man enveloped in a long black cloak, who wore a sun-mask of black velvet tied over his features. And we knew we were looking upon the executioner.

The Marshal said to him: "I have a lad here who shall make out your bill and mine. Are you satisfied?"

The executioner said he was, in a low, husky voice which he seemed trying to disguise.

"Well," said Mr. Gullet, "here are the jail keys": and handed them to the masked creature. "Will you go and look over your prisoners now?" he added.

The executioner murmured that he desired to sleep first for an hour because he was very weary from his long journey.

The Marshal nodded. "To turn off five men and a woman," said he, "is no easy job; and if you have come a-horse from Virginia and have travelled all night, you had best bespeak a bed-chamber and sleep until I summon you."

The tap-boy came with materials for writing, and the Marshal asked him where the executioner might find a bed for an hour's repose.

Instantly it came into my mind to contrive some way of using this dreadful fellow; yet had no clear purpose in my thought when I offered the executioner my own chamber and my own bed to lie on if he would pay me sixpence in silver.

As I spoke I rested my hand on Paul West's knee and pinched it hard.

"Here," said Mr. Gullet, "is a silver sixpence, and a silver shilling in advance for your writing." And he laid the money before me, and I put it in my pocket.

So the tap-boy took the executioner away and up the stairs to my chamber whilst I made ready to write what Mr. Gullet might wish. And this is what

I wrote for him as he spoke it:

Bill of Noah Gullet

The Proprietors of North Carolina to Noah Gullet, Marshal, for sundrys by him expended by order of a special Court of Admiralty, for the execution of six Pirates; viz.:

To the making of the chains for Pedro Sangsue, William Hope, James Cutler, Tom Gryme, Edmund Cawley, and Mary Read	£18	10	9
To the executioner for his services	£20	00	0
To Uriah Ropes for cordage	£3	6	6
To setting gibbets	£1	9	10
To digging three graves (Hope, Gryme, and Sansue to rot where they hang)	£1	6	0
To tavern expenses for Provost, sheriff, Constables, after the execution (allowed)	£6	0	0

When I had written this, I added the total account and offered the ink-wet sheet to Mr. Gullet.

So he sanded it and took it away with him to show to the Governor.

Now, no sooner had he gone out of the tavern than I whispered to Paul West what plan I had designed while writing, and bade him go instantly to the mews and there hire two saddle horses, and pay for them, and ride one—leading the other—to the edge of the oak woods behind the jail.

"For, by the martydrom of my blessed Saviour," said I in a white heat of excitement, "I mean to take from the executioner his keys, though God only knows how it is to be accomplished!"

Paul West was trembling so he could scarce stand, but I pushed him out the door, then ran back and sped past the till where the fat tap-boy was again asleep, and so up the stairs, cat-foot, and stole swiftly to my chamber door and pried it open without a sound.

On my bed lay a little old, withered man, asleep in his shirt and breeches; and his crooked, naked feet sprawled across the blanket. He snored and snored, lying flat upon his back; and he did not stir when I took his great, black cloak and his mask and the keys which lay upon a stool.

The next instant I was out o' the room, and had tied the mask over my face, dragged down my beaver, wrapped me in the cloak, and, carrying the ring with its iron keys, hastened down the stairs.

The jail stood on Carteret Road. To gain it I passed by Rosebud Lane, by Princess Lane, by Charles Street, and into the jail road where were only two houses and some barns besides the jail.

The few folk I met abroad shrank away from me in my dark cloak and vizard; but it was in the heat o' the day, and people remained indoors for the most.

However, I met two soldiers going toward the jail, who stared at me with lively curiosity, and I heard them jesting after I passed them and wondering aloud who Jack Ketch might really be.

The jail was small and built of peeled logs smeared with blue clay. It seemed no stronger than one of those log forts which are built by the poor folk who venture to make homes for themselves in the Indian country on our unexplored frontiers.

The jailor, with a musket on his knee, sat in the shadow of the front door, which was open to the breeze. A blanket divided the hallway midway between the front door and the transverse corridor.

When the jailor saw me, he took his clay pipe from his mouth, laid the musket aside, bade me good day, and inquired how he could serve me best.

"By minding your own business," said I in a gruff and altered voice; and went into the jail flourishing and clanking my keys and twirling them on the iron ring.

The cell corridor which ran east and west across the hallway was, as I say, divided from the front door by a dirty blanket which hung there, so that the jailor could not see the rear door from where he sat on guard.

There were ten cells in the corridor, the doors of which were barred high up, so that I had to stand on tip-toe to see into each cell as I passed along. And, in the last cell on my left I discovered Mary Read, seated upon a truss of trampled straw.

She wore no longer her gay, scarlet vest and breeches, and her chains and kerchief and silken sash with its pistols and daggers. She wore a poor woman's dress of blue cotton cloth; her pretty hair fell thick about her face which was calm but very colourless. Upon her feet were Indian moccasins.

When she heard me trying the lock with several keys ere I chanced upon the right one, her face altered and flushed; and she stood up quickly in her cell, staring at my masked visage through the bars.

The other pirates who, when I entered, had been very silent in their cells, now began to stir in their straw and stand up, hearing the noise of keys, and I heard them calling to one another by name to inquire what was to do, and if their hour had arrived.

When, at last, I unlocked and unbarred the door, I stepped swiftly into the little cell.

"Mary Read," I whispered.

At that she gave me a wild look; and I lifted my mask a moment, then tied it fast again.

"Paul waits among the live oaks with horses," I whispered. "So get you to the woods, in God's name.... And carry with you in your heart the love of a young girl who always will pray for you and the man you love!"

Even then, where she stood at the very door of death, she revealed her true and generous self; for she took me into her arms and looked at me out of her beautiful brown eyes.

"And shall you come to harm for this, my pretty?" she asked. "For I will not take my life of you and injure yours."

I told her I was secure, and drew her to the rear door where, on the wood's edge, I could see two horses standing under the live oaks and a man astride one o' them.

Then she turned and clasped me to her breast, and kissed and kissed me, uttering not a word. And so left me, and ran toward the trees where, in a moment more, she vanished.

Until I saw her mounted upon a horse, and galloping northward beside her lover, I did not stir. Then I went swiftly and opened wide her cell door, while a dreadful stillness reigned among those lost men in their barred cells—all listening in breathless silence to learn if their doom already were upon them.

"Jailor!" I shouted as harshly as I could force a voice which naturally is low and soft. And when he came a-clumping, and, pushing aside the blanket, discovered me, I made him a sign for silence. Then, taking him by the sleeve, I drew him to Mary Read's cell.

"The five men are here," said I. "Where is the woman?"

He gaped at the empty cell like the dumb gaby he was; then stared at me out of round and frightened eyes, and his toothless jaws sagged wide.

"Where is your turnkey?" I whispered.

"Asleep in his quarters.... Oh, my God—"

I placed my mouth at his ear: "She's gone!" said I. "And lest there be a general jail delivery planned at this hour, make no noise but rouse your fellow and stand guard by these cells until I come again with the Provost Marshal, Noah Gullet. Do you understand?"

He nodded, unable to utter a word.

So, leaving him, I went out again by the front door, and hastened through a cow lane into an alley which presently fetched me to the tavern mews, and so, by the rear door, into the Eden Arms.

Not a sound in the tavern; all was deathly still, and the tap-boy asleep behind the spindles.

Cat-foot I mounted the stairs. The door of my bed-chamber stood open. The hangman lay upon my bed as I had left him, unstirring in the deep stupor of his sleep.

I laid his cloak and vizard and keys where I had found them; then, on tip-toe, crept out, closed the door noiselessly behind me, and descended to the taproom and sat down by the table in the corner where I had sat but a little while before with the despairing lover of Mary Read.

And now, finally, I began to be frightened, and fell a-shivering where I sat, striving to consider what was to happen when the flight of Mary Read had been discovered.

The stillness in the tavern began to terrify me. Through the silence which seemed like a hollow noise roaring in my brain, the tall, square-topped clock ticked and ticked like the continuous cocking of pistols. My fear-wide eyes were fixed on its polished case— following the infinite vermiculation of its inlaid figures of king-wood and satin-wood which were designs of vines and flowers; and here and there a grotesque human figure.

I know not how long I lay there upon my chair before I became conscious that, outside the tavern, the town of Edenton was waking up.

First, distantly, I heard the noise of an iron bell, not very loud, but it sounded sadly and at long intervals, and was tolling as though for a passing soul.

Presently there were voices in the street and along the water-front; horsemen trotted past; folk spoke loudly; women called to one another; a noise of hammering came from the wharf below the water-stairs.

Now, as I sat there, I heard men coming into the entry, and the sound of many voices and of heavy boots.

Presently, into the taproom stepped Noah Gullet, the Provost, and with him a large, fierce fellow and three others. These, I learned, were the Sheriff of Albemarle and his constables, for, when Mr. Gullet awoke the fat tap-boy, he so addressed them.

"Now, my fat and porky lad," says Gullet, rubbing his large, flabby hands, "go you up and awake old Jack Ketch," says he, "for, dammy and curse my lights-and-liver," says he, "there is to be a very pretty hanging holden upon Eden sands this lovely summer day!" And, seeing me, he winked upon me.

So the tap-boy went upstairs to awaken the executioner and when he came back, Mr. Gullet commanded a bowl of punch for all, and, while it was a-brewing, a can of flip to stay the company.

To me he said: "You sleepy young rogue, you gouged a shilling and sixpence out o' me, and you shall pay for what you guzzle, and be damned to you!"

"Be damned to yourself," said I, "and take your money to buy you a little schooling—you letterless lout!"

"Why, you impudent pup—" he roared, but I threw his money upon the sanded floor, and got up and went out the door.

On the sill, pausing to listen, I heard the executioner a-coming with his keys, clink, clink down the stairs. It was time for me to go if I wished to avoid what must come very quickly, now.

As I stepped into the street I heard a drum beating, and saw, in Princess Lane, a company of soldiers wearing red coats, white breeches and black gaiters, and led by a drummer and an officer.

Everywhere, from every street, lane and alley, people were now arriving in flocks, all moving toward the riverfront from whence came a steady and loud sound of hammering. Children crowded about the troops, running alongside the moving ranks and following the rear of the column where a small body of horse rode with their gorgets, spurs, and naked swords shining in the rosy light of the declining sun.

As I went out and mingled with the increasing throngs, I saw the Provost Marshal, the Sheriff, and the constables come from the tavern, all a-wiping of their lips and chins and smacking their tongues.

These fell in behind the horsemen. Then, dub-dub-rub-dub-dub! rattled the long, painted drum, and the procession set out up Princess Lane toward the jail.

Some people followed; but the majority hurried to the river where they took places above and all around the Execution Dock where carpenters were still working upon the gallows.

As for me, I had no stomach left to endure so horrid a sight. To see living men turned off—even these bloody sea-rogues—was more than I could stand.

So, not knowing what to do, and yet fearful of inviting suspicion, I followed the throng that was marching to the jail.

It had already arrived there when I came up and instantly I saw there was a commotion at the jail, and heard loud voices in anger and dispute. For the jailor was swearing *sacrement* that the hangman had already been there that very day, and that he had discovered the delivery of the female pirate, Mary Read, and had ordered the jailor and the turnkey to stand guard over the other pirates until the executioner returned.

To which the masked hangman gave him the lie in an astonished voice, and swore that he had slept at the Eden Arms upon a bed, and had never waked until the tap-boy summoned him half an hour ago.

Every instant the uproar increased, what with the angry bawling of the Provost who threatened everybody with the Governor's displeasure; the profane abuse of the Sheriff cursing the Provost, the jailor, the turnkey, and his own constables; and the stern and sarcastic voice of the Captain of Horse who offered his opinion regarding all civil servants of Government, and added that the only government for so lousy a province as Carolina was a military one.

There seemed to be no clergyman there, only a kind of dissenting minister who strove to quiet the tumult and who went in, presently, to the condemned men followed by the cursing turnkey and the constables.

The prisoners were led out with their hands tied behind their backs, which, I heard people saying to one another, was unusual; and that their hands should be tied before them.

God knows why it mattered; but one of the condemned men shouted to the Sheriff that he stood upon his rights and desired to be hanged fashionably.

At which a dreadful laughter arose; and the pirates, as they passed under guard, jested horridly with the crowds, so utterly hardened and unrepentant were these sea-wolves of Captain Rackham's company.

One young man shouted out that he had been warned that he would, one day, die in his boots.

"A cursed lie!" he cried, "as all may witness!"—and kicked the two tattered shoes from his feet, and marched on barefoot, stepping high and playing the clown to the solemn tap of the drum.

As for the minister, they derided him and would have none of him; and the poor man trudged along trying to read aloud the prayers for the dying while these six sea-rogues mocked and mimicked him and jested foully among themselves.

I stood and watched that shocking and contemptible procession pass; and saw it winding on far away in the red sunset light, and heard the distant throb of the drum timing that grotesque death-march.

Then, all alone, past houses emptied of their curious inmates, past silent lane and empty alley and still, deserted streets, I moved until I came to Eden Hall.

And there, by the rear garden gate, went in, and stood among the flowers, silent, weary, wondering concerning God and the strange mystery of His purpose with men, and with the sons of men.

CHAPTER VI
ALL FLAGS!

From the tavern door I heard a voice, saying to the landlord of the Eden Arms:

"I am looking for a thin, yellow-haired, freckled boy who came from Topsail Inlet to wait upon Governor Eden."

The burly landlord came to the taproom window, which was open, and poked his fat face inside.

"Freckles," says he to me, "Colonel Rhett inquires for you."

I got up from the settle and went outside, and saw a handsome young gentleman, very elegantly dressed, sitting upon a fine gray mare by the horse-block. So I pulled off my new beaver hat to him, and was very glad that it was new and thrice cocked.

I don't know why he was amused at me.

"Good morning," said he gaily; "I regret that I forget your name, my son, but I remember your freckled description. You are the boy called Freckles, I suppose?"

"Yes, sir."

"Servant to Tom Cocklyn, landlord of Lost Ship Tavern at Topsail Inlet?"

"Yes, sir."

"Very well," said he, smilingly, "hop up on my horse behind, me and I will carry you to Governor Eden who has news for you."

He was so handsome, so gay, so fashionably attired, that, being a girl—though all the world supposed I was a lad—it pleased me to be seen riding pillion behind so gallant a horseman.

So I scrambled up behind him and clasped both my thin arms around his body; and the beautiful horse moved out along the river in a sort of dancing step as though happy to carry us.

"So," says he, "you are tap-boy to old Tom Cocklyn who is the greatest rogue unhung between Cape Fear and Currituck."

He laughed when he said it, and I laughed too, as he turned his head to look at me over his be-ribboned shoulder.

Says he, speaking now more gravely: "Governor Eden tells me you are only child to the late Captain Topsfield whom Israel Hornygold, the pirate, murdered on the high seas, and then most barbarously burned, together with your mother and the plundered ship."

"Yes, sir," said I in a low voice.

"Do you know who I am, Freckles?"

"Are you the same Colonel Rhett who sailed northward in chase of the sea-rogue, Charles Vane?"

"I am. And your friend, Mr. Ross, in the *Moth*, sloop-tender, sailed in my company. And he told me of his esteem and affection for yourself."

I went hot, then cold, then became voiceless, choked with an emotion so new, so deep, that it left me dumb and bewildered.

"Charles Vane escaped us," said he. "I think he sailed south, and am following him. But if I do not discover him this side Cape Fear, then I shall return to Ocracoke Inlet and search for that great fool, Stede Bonnet, who is too ignorant to navigate and too vain to admit it."

"And—and Mr. Ross, sir," I ventured; "will he return here presently?"

"He and I parted off the Virginia Capes, and he stood for Maryland, hoping to find Jack Rackham cruising in those waters. But I think that Calico Jack sailed south again.... And may even pay a call on your master, Tom Cocklyn, at Topsail Inlet."

We now had arrived at the Governor's mansion, and I slipped off the horse and ran to hold Mr. Rhett's stirrup as he descended.

"You are a well-mannered youngster," said he, and gave me sixpence, for which civility I thanked him as politely as I knew how.

"Well, Freckles," said he, in his smiling way, "I know something of your history, and hope better things for you than to serve Tom Cocklyn as a tavern drudge. So fare you well, my lad, and serve

God and Governor Eden and Mr. Ross; and between the three you should reap a reward of some kind."

He was laughing when he rode away. I took off my new beaver hat to him, and he waved his gloved hand—from the silken cuff of which floated ruffles of blond lace as exquisite as patterned cobwebs.

Being a girl and no boy, I notice such matters to admire them, and all apparel which is costly, which I conceive to be a very innocent inclination and not sinful vanity.

Well, I went to the door and knocked, and a servant in yellow livery, piped, faced, and turned up with purple, opened for me; and, no doubt having been averted by the Governor, conducted me up the stairs and into a pretty bedroom.

"Master Topsfield," said he, "his Excellency desires you to lodge here instead of at the Eden Arms, until such time as Mr. Ross can return in his sloop to carry you back to Topsail Inlet."

I was so astonished that I sat down upon the bed's edge and gazed dumbly upon the footman.

He said, speaking with a sort of disdainful kindness, but wrinkling his long and pointed nose at me as though sniffing an odour not perfectly agreeable:

"His Excellency desires that you signify to me when you wish to eat; and your food will be served to you in your bed-chamber."

That was far too much for me who, when fed at all, had been contented with a crust and a cheese-rind in Tom Cocklyn's ratty pantry.

I muttered that any food would be acceptable; and then my eyes, travelling about the room, noticed a Chinese box standing near the bed's foot; and could smell the perfumed lacquer of it and the sandalwood.

To this box the footman now walked majestically, opened it, and displayed, within it, a suit of silken clothing, shirts, drawers of madras, clocked stockings of silk, pretty buckled shoes and—oh, heaven!—a little looking glass, a cake of scented soap in a box, an iron to curl gentlemen's hair, a comb, scissors, and a box of pomade which, when opened, filled the whole room with an elegant rose-like odour.

Never before, I think, had any lad—much less a girl disguised as one—possessed so beautiful a wardrobe of clothing and such fashionable necessaries which were suitable for a young gentleman of quality, but scarcely for a ragged pot-boy in Tom Cocklyn's tavern.

I said to the footman in a voice which trembled a little:

"May I wait upon his Excellency Governor Eden to thank him?"

"His Excellency," said he, with his nose in the air, "permits you to approach him in his plaisaunce."

"What is that?" I inquired.

He gave me a glance of suffering patience. "His Excellency's flower-garden," he explained. And then he marched away down the stairs: and I fell upon my knees to examine and caress the clothing in this wonder-box.

On my wash-stand was a big earthen pitcher in a large glazed bowl. So I filled the bowl with water, stripped off my clothes, and, with my scented soap, bathed me until I smelled as fresh and sweet as a garden. Next I trimmed me and curled my hair.

Then, dressing in my silken suit, I ran down the stairs and out into the garden, where, beyond the drifting fountain spray, I discovered Governor Eden seated in a willow chair, reading a book called *The Art of War*.

To him I went, trying not to run or hasten at any unseemly gait; and, when near him, removed my new beaver hat and made him my manners very carefully.

He looked up with that haggard smile of his; indicated a stool near him; and I bowed to him again and seated myself, and instantly expressed, as politely as I knew how, my undying gratitude for his bounty.

"Freckles," said he, wanly amused, "Colonel Rhett fetched that box of clothing in his sloop out of Virginia; and, for it, you are beholden to Mr. Ross, and not to me."

My heart began to beat violently, and I felt the swift heat burn my face at mention of Mr. Ross's name.

His Excellency said: "Mr. Ross seems very particular concerning you, Freckles; and he sends word to me by Mr. Rhett that it would infinitely oblige him if I offer you a chamber under my roof until he can return to take you aboard the *Moth*.... And so I have done so."

I managed to thank his Excellency again, who looked at me out of kind but melancholy eyes in a sort of sad approval.

"Your manners are genteel, my boy," said he, "and do credit to the worthy sea-captain whose son you are.... And also, no doubt, to the careful training of a devoted mother.... One matter is becoming clear to me—that to serve in the taproom of The Lost Ship is no fit business for a lad like you."

He considered me in silence for a while. "Tom Cocklyn is a rascal," he said. "He is an old pirate, and took advantage of the Royal proclamation to receive the King's pardon. But old pirates never die honest men. Sooner or later Tom Cocklyn will take the sea again. As do all such pious rogues who once have seen the gallows' shadow, and have taken fright at it and crawled into sanctuary.... I know them, Freckles.... It is fear that turns them honest, not repentance.... Fear does not last. It cannot. Fear kills; or it fades, dies out, and is forgotten.... Freckles?"

"Sir?"

"Fear is the cruellest and most dreadful affliction that ever besets mankind. No suffering, no torture on earth, can compare to its atrocity.... Many will tell you that love is the most powerful of human emotions; others maintain that hate is more powerful still.... But *I* tell you that fear is far more formidable than either, and rules more subjects than do love and hate ... and is a punishment so terrible that no threat of hell hereafter is as awful as the hell in which man's living mind agonizes under the grip of fear."

My curious gaze was fastened upon this man's strained and pallid face; and my natural surprise changed to consternation as I saw his worn features alter and become ashen and haggard while he spoke to me concerning fear.

I think his emotion carried him farther than he meant, and that he now read as much in my expression, for he checked himself and forced a mirthless smile; but I saw how painful was the effort.

"Well," said he, "this is a solemn discourse for so lovely a day under these soft skies of Carolina. So think no more of such ugly things as fear and death, Freckles, and let us employ these gentle hours in profitable pleasures.... For me, a book is the happiest refuge from care. In my library are books; and, if you are neat, and understanding, and handle them with caution and clean fingers, you may go thither and choose for yourself a volume to amuse you."

I promised fervently; and, asking his leave, jumped up and ran into the house, and came to the library where was an array of books that astonished and excited me.

After long search and delicious hesitations, I chose a book called *The Secrets of Cathay*; and crept to my bedroom with it; and there, seated upon the bed, very delicately opened and turned the wondrous pages.

It was one of the happiest days of my life; and sometimes I read in my book and sometimes let my eyes wander over my new silken breeches and stockings, and, again, touched the silver buckles on my new shoes to admire them.

Thought wandered; my lost gaze roved about the sunny bedroom where flowered curtains stirred in jasmine-scented winds; and I thought ardently of Mr. Ross until, under my fine new shirt and my small breasts, my heart became very violent.

At noonday, feeling hungry, I went timidly to the lower floor and there asked a servant if I might have a little food.

Oh, heaven! They fetched to my chamber upon a lacquered tray a young roasted pigeon upon a couch of honeyed rice, a salad, oranges and guavas in thick cream, and a large canary-tinted goblet of cut glass full of white muscat wine called muscadel, and scented like a garden.

When they removed the Chinese serving tray I was completely full of this exquisite nourishment, and felt of my body complacently, hoping that I was becoming a little rounder, and ran a little less to ribs.

Hearing a man's rough and very vulgar voice in the garden below, I went to the window and looked down between the curtains.

There was the Honourable Charles Eden, our Governor, seated under a magnolia tree; and, near him, upon the settle, squatted a huge and hairy man. He was the most remarkable looking man that ever I had laid eyes upon, brutally built, yet in shambling fashion and not well proportioned. His legs seemed somewhat weak and short, but his arms were muscular and enormous. Above his belly, which was a paunch, a mighty chest and neck supported a head which was much too small and wizened, and would have seemed like the hideous and withered head of an idiot only for the amazing growth of hair and beard upon it.

The hair was thick and greasy-black, and fell upon his shoulders. But the beard—oh, my God!—it sprouted under his eyes and covered all his face, coarse as a horse's tail, and was braided into a score of little pig-tails, each of which was tied with a bow of different coloured ribbon. Two of these greasy braids he wore looped over his ears, which stood wide of his head and were extremely large and thin and full of blood vessels.

Never had I gazed upon a human creature so instantly and completely offensive to my eyes.

And that, although his apparel was truly magnificent. From his wide ears hung great jewelled hoops; his thick fingers were crowded with rings; fathoms of gold-linked chains embraced his neck. And, as for the rest, he wore a laced shirt of finest lawn, vest and wide sea-pants of cherry coloured silk, and a kind of skirted jerkin of cloth of gold over a green and orange sash.

Into that sash were thrust two Moor's daggers in hammered gold sheaths; and these were the only weapons in his sash. But, from his shoulder-belt, hung six silk cords; and from each cord dangled a pistol!

Now, there was no need for me to wonder who this fearsome man might be; I knew instantly and recognized him from descriptions upon many a tavern notice, and many a broadside and printed ballad.

For this monster could be no other than Edward Teach, sometimes called Ned Thatch, and known generally as Black-Beard, the wickedest, cruellest, boldest, and most impudent pirate who ever harried Carolina.

Now, what on earth was this great rogue doing in our Governor's garden?—talking to his Excellency with boisterous familiarity, roaring with mirth, devouring food, guzzling wine, pulling at his long pipe amid vast clouds of smoke, cursing, damning, spitting, using language so foul and lewd that I will not deprave my page by setting it down.

The Governor sat there, deathly white, sunk back deep in his willow arm-chair—a strange, crushed, tragic figure, striving to make some countenance to this impudent villain, even trying to smile. Oh, holy angels! what a sight there on the grass among the magnolia trees and pretty flowers in the sunny splendour of the afternoon!

Now, suddenly, both men turned their heads; and there came past the garden, along a gravel road, a company of sea-rogues in their gaudy finery, barefoot, half-naked, and every man rolling before him a great hogshead of sugar which they stowed in a storehouse near to the blacks' quarters—hogshead after hogshead, dozen after dozen, all of vast value in Carolina, until I had counted sixty.

When the last of the sugar was stowed away and the sea-wolves had departed along the gravel road, Mr. Teach got up out of his chair and clapped Mr. Eden upon his shoulder and seemed in a monstrous fine humour, though the Governor gazed at him like a dead man.

Then his Excellency also rose, and together they came toward the house. I heard them below, talking together; then up the stairs they came, still in conversation, and into the room adjoining mine, which was the Governor's privy study, although I did not know it then.

Whether the Governor thought I was in the library, or even remembered me at all, I do not know; for, although he spoke in a strained tone and low, Mr. Teach roared and bellowed with no discretion whatever; and, what was said, I could scarcely avoid hearing, even if I had wished to close my ears.

Never did I listen to such horrid cursing and damning and

swearing and foul words as interlarded nearly every phrase this filthy pirate uttered; yet, he was not at all angry, but merely in most excellent humour—and seemed to banter Mr. Eden, jesting at his expense in a fashion which made me wonder if he had some dreadful kind of power over this pale and delicately nurtured gentleman of quality and refinement.

"God curse my eyes!" says he, "why should I fear Alec Spottswood of Virginia when I have so staunch a friend in you, Charles Eden? Why should I concern myself with that damned old buzzard, Nick Trott—or with Rhett—or with Charles-Town—God blast the hell-spawned city!"

"I pray you, moderate your voice, Mr. Teach," interposed the Governor.

"Dammy, why should I? I care not who knows I'm here in Edenton—or who knows that my ship is here *to take all flags!* Why should I care when I am protected by the Honourable Charles Eden, Governor of—"

"Would you shout it from the house-tops and bring me to ruin, Mr. Teach?"

"I? Ruin you! Not all the devils in hell and all the she-devils who cook souls in hell's kitchen could force me to do you an unkindness who are friendly to poor old Edward Teach, and will ever protect him against all the cursed navies of the American Colonies and all the damnable station-ships of the hell-born Royal Navy in North America!"

He was plainly in boisterous and mirthful spirits; he hummed, he spat, he burst out into vile songs and snatches, and made a shuffling noise with his painted boot-heels as though dancing.

"Well," says he, "I have fetched you sixty barrel of sugar, two pipe of Madeira, two of Oporto, twelve bales of figured, striped, and plain India silks, five bars of refined Arab gold, and fifteen keg of Morocco silver."

"I tell you," said Mr. Eden in a low, tense voice, "I wish none of these—"

"And *I* tell *you* that you shall have them!" roared Teach, "because you have earned them; and I always pay my reckoning! It is too late, your Excellency, for you to sicken of our bargain, or ever to deny it. You shall hold fast to it; and so shall I, by God! When I sail, I sail to take all flags! And you shall remember that any man who takes my ship and me, takes, with both these, enough evidence to ruin and beggar you and send you to London Tower!"

Mr. Eden said in the ghost of a voice: "I have no intention of playing you false. I ask only that you leave these parts and operate elsewhere—"

"Damnation!" yelled Teach. "I operate where it suits me! I will have you understand that I am a man who does always what pleases him. I take any and all flags, and spare only a black or bloody one. I kill where I choose—whom I choose; I slay when offended; I slay sometimes for pleasure and when not at all offended—"

"Will you moderate your tones?"

"Listen, damn you! Two weeks since I took a Portuguese muletta, off the Virginia Capes. He had not offended me. Do you know what I did to him? I sliced off his nose, both ears, both lips, and my cook fried them, and I made the Portugee captain eat his own ears and nose and lips, and then shot him in the bowels because I ordered him to smack his lips, but he had none to smack!—"

Such hellish laughter I never before heard as the awful mirth which burst from the maw of Mr. Teach.

"I'll tell you another joke," he cried; "I had all my officers to wine in my cabin; and when all were very merry I pulled two pistols and, crossing them, closed my eyes and fired at random. And my quartermaster fell dead and my mate lost a leg which went green on him—oh, my God!—" he was suffocating with laughter, and stamping with his boots and slapping his thighs.

When he was a little recovered: "Well," says he, "I leave you, Charles Eden; but first shall tell you where I design to go and what I mean to do. I shall sail to Charles-Town in South Carolina to take all flags and all nations. And there seize upon such shipping as I discover in the harbour; and show to the city my four flags which are my black colours, a bloody ensign at the main, a black pennant, and a death-jack.

"Then, by God, I shall go ashore, and ruffle it in the streets of Charles-Town; and I shall have out of that city a fine chest of medicines worth a thousand pounds or more; and shall not pay a farthing for it, but, if refused, will hang every man, woman, and child aboard what prizes I have taken, and you shall hear Charles-Town howling a hundred miles as you sit below in your pretty garden!"

"If you do that," said the Governor in a ghastly voice, "all North America will rise against you."

"If you betray my purpose to a living soul," roared Black-Beard, "you share my fate! Otherwise," he cried with a dreadful laugh, "let all North America set sail and chase me and be cursed and damned to them and to the whole damned world beside!"

I heard him get up from a chair, and the floor creaked under his weighty bulk as he walked to the door.

"Adieu, Charles," he said. "For your silence, when I come again to Edenton, I bring you costly presents. Women, too, if you choose. No? Well then, my taste is different; for I have married twenty wives, and have ruined some, tortured some, made sows of others, and cut the throats of the rest. And, in two days more, I shall marry my twenty-first—she is only sixteen—when I arrive at Topsail Inlet. And, having sported with her, shall deliver her to my crew for their amusement—"

"You filthy dog!" said the Governor, "who is it you mean to marry at Topsail Inlet?"

"Well, I'll tell you that, too, Charles. There's a yellow-haired and freckled tap-boy who serves Tom Cocklyn's guests in his tavern there; and Francis Farrington Sprigg had it from Israel Hornygold— before Ross took him—that this same tap-boy is no boy at all, but a girl in boy's clothing; and was Captain Topsfield's child, whom Hornygold burned in his own ship, the *Fancy Nancy*.

"And that's my twenty-first bride-to-be, Charles—and God help her when I'm through with her!"

Never a word answered the Governor. And so, presently, and loud in mirth, Mr. Teach went a-clumping down the stairway, stamping through the hall below until the noise of him grew distant and died away when the front door closed behind him.

But, in the street outside, he paused to turn and yell back at the silent house:

"All flags, by God, and all nations!"

Then silence fell upon that doomed mansion.

I would not vaunt myself, yet may say this much, that it was concern and fear and pity for Mr. Eden, and no terror for myself, that urged me to run to his Excellency in the adjoining room. Where I discovered him huddled in a deep chair, crushed, speechless as a dead man.

Down upon my knees I dropped and took his thin hand and kissed it; and he lifted his head to stare at me out of sunken eyes that seemed blinded.

"Sir," I said, "what indiscretion you may have committed I know not, and am very ignorant of; but I know that you have been loved by our good folk of Carolina in days gone by, and are reputed to be greatly approved by his Majesty the King of England; and therefore must be both honourable and good. And so I am come to assure your Excellency of a poor servant's faith and loyalty and love, which is all the gift I have to offer you."

He leaned forward, presently, and, taking me by the shoulders, kissed me on both cheeks, which amazing honour astounded me.

"So you heard all," said he.... "I had forgotten you.... And did you listen, also, to what this fellow said concerning you?"

"Yes, sir."

"Is it true that you are a girl and no boy, Freckles?"

"Yes, sir."

After a silence: "Can your Excellency attempt nothing against this known pirate?" I asked.

But he gave me the heartbroken look of a damned man, and I knew he must be, somehow, entangled and in that monster's power.

Now I understood something of that worldly hell called Fear, of which this wretched man had lately spoken. But such a passion of love and pity for him overwhelmed me that I began to weep, and caress his hands.

"Let me help," I sobbed. "I can, perhaps, entrap this common enemy of mankind at Topsail Inlet, and set a signal for the station-ships to take him—"

"Child," said he, "would you chance the horror with which you heard him threaten you?"

"As for that, sir," I replied, "I can fend for myself who have learned cunning sufficient to survive every violence and starvation—"

"No. My God, no!" said he. Then he rose and began to pace the floor.

"It has come to a pass," said he, "where I cannot go on. Whatever betide, I cannot go on in this fashion—"

He turned on me: "Once," said he, "when ruin threatened and I needed money, I was tempted. And trafficked with pirates—with Edward Teach; and with Tom Cocklyn.... And these have blackmailed* me ever since.... No; I cannot go on in this manner.... Already there is suspicion of me in Carolina that I do nothing to stop Edward Teach in his impudence and plundering, yet hang others who are caught sailing On The Account.... Oh, God, if I only knew how to come at this monster and not perish with him in his ruin—"

"Sir," I cried, "will you call on the Governor of Virginia?"

"I dare not send any man out of Carolina on such a mission which must utterly condemn me in my own colony if it become known."

He began to pace the room again like a hunted creature.

"Sir, may *I* go?" I cried.

At that he turned on his heel and came toward me, taking both my hands. A pale hope flared in his faded eyes.

"What would you say to Governor Spottswood?" he demanded.

---

* Black-Beard surrendered to the King's proclamation and was given a certificate by Governor Eden. Which was lawful. But Black-Beard had taken an English vessel in piracy, pretending she was Spanish. The blackmail dated from the Court of Vice-Admiralty which adjudicated unjustly this prize to Black-Beard at Bath-Town.

"I would say that Carolina cannot cope with this monster unaided."

I felt his hands tighten over mine, cling to them.

"How would you go to him?" he whispered.

"Give me a horse."

"The Tuscarora Indians would murder you."

"Then give me a sloop!"

"You must go alone."

"A pinnace, then, with lateen! A canoe—anything!—for I am bred to the sea, sir, and never have feared it in all my life!"

"I cannot ask it—"

"You need not, sir, for I offer first, and beg it, now, as a favour."

At that his wasted features quivered and he sat down on his chair and took his head between his hands.

I ran to my room, dressed me in the wool clothes given me by Mr. Ross, laid away my finery in the Chinese box, and came again to his Excellency.

"Sir," said I, "have a care for my beautiful garments which I have laid away again in the lacquered box. And give me a little minted money, if you please, so that I lose no instant, but run to the water-stairs and hire me a canoe, and provision it, and so get me into Virginia as soon as may be."

He seemed dazed; but he took a heavy purse of gold from his pocket and gave it.

"When I come again," said I, "I hope to come aboard Mr. Ross in the *Moth*, tender. And if I miss him, then I shall come aboard any craft Virginia may send us to take this great villain, called Black-Beard, in all his wickedness."

He sprang up, took me in his arms and kissed me. Then he sat down with his face in both hands, and I saw the great tears falling between his fingers.

Well, I left him, and ran to the water-stairs, and there, for six pieces of eight, I hired me a canoe of a Minorcan water-man, which craft had also a lateen to hoist when needed.

Then to the Eden Arms, where I borrowed a chart and a compass; and purchased and stowed away in my canoe a sack of hard bread and a great cheese, a candle, a hatchet, a hank of spare cord, six fathoms of rope, flints, tinder, a brass pistol, a horn o' powder, bullets in a bag, and a little can of priming powder. This, with sweet water in a little cask, I stowed aboard.

There was a fine, bright wind on the river. I hoisted sail and sped away like a very swallow across the sound, Kitty Hawk bearing dead ahead. All night long I sailed; and so into Currituck; and, next day, out the inlet and around False Cape. The third day, by the Virginia Capes I sped to the great reaches of the James, near dying of weariness, having slept only at the tiller with one eye on the sheet.

And, here on the lower river, I raised a sail which presently I made out to be a sloop. Then, oh, heavenly angels! a wild surmise excited me, and I made all sail to overhaul this vessel, and loaded and fired my pistol till it became too hot to handle.

For now I knew it was the *Moth* I chased, and was swiftly intercepting.

When I came near, the mast-head hailed me, and I sobbed out Mr. Ross's name. So near insensible was I that when they lifted me on deck I could scarce see or speak, only seemed to know when *his* arms cradled me and carried me below.

"Nancy," he whispered, "Nancy Topsfield."

I roused me with a last effort.

"Before I sleep," said I, "this is the best news I have out of Carolina; that Edward Teach has sailed to take *all flags!* And stands for Charles-Town. And Governor Eden calls Virginia to Carolina's aid!"

"You poor and gallant child," says he in infinite pity, "Carolina, fearing her own Governor, hath already sent petitions to Alexander Spottswood. And Virginia takes the sea."

"Oh, God," I whimpered, "then our Governor is undone and his heart and honour break!"

My brain swam: I laid my head against Mr. Ross's breast to steady me.

"Help him," I whispered.

"If he be guilty—"

"He is. But God forgives him. And so shall you.... Sir, will you stand for Charles-Town?"

"Yes," he whispered, "or for anywhere on earth you wish—Nancy Topsfield."

I smiled, and my lips parted to speak words I never uttered, as every sense within me succumbed, deep drowned in sleep.

CHAPTER VII
THE CRAZY JADE

When the *Moth*, sloop-tender to his Majesty's station-ship *Sea-Hawk*, Captain Sir George Sayles, came to an anchor in Topsail Inlet, I had but just finished dressing me in my boy's wool clothing where I had slept in the flag-locker.

I had no baggage. I was quite ready to go ashore as soon as I could find the master.

Mr. Ross I waited upon very gaily in his cabin, who was master of the *Moth*.

"Well, Nancy," he began, but I bade him sharply to have a care how he spoke to me lest his crew learn that I was no boy, but a girl in boy's clothing. Which might undo me if known at Topsail Inlet, and if Tom Cocklyn heard of it.

"Nobody is listening," said he, "except a mouse or two."

"I would not have a ship's mouse know the truth," said I. However, I smiled upon him; but his smile died; and the more soberly he gazed upon me the gayer my smile.

"Freckles," says he in a sorrowful tone, "do you leave me then so gaily?"

At that I laughed; and, setting the toe of one foot flat upon the cabin floor, spun my body around. For my spirits were become as light as my heels, though he never guessed why.

And it was all because my girl's heart was telling me that, in this young man's bosom, a kind of tenderness for me was taking root more deeply every day. And God knows how light it made my heart and heels to discover it.

"Freckles," says he, "you are a heartless baggage."

"Be pleased," said I, "to stow that same baggage in the pinnace and set it ashore."

"You vex me," said he, giving me a glum look. O Lord, how light it made my heels to see him troubled at my going.

So that I fairly danced on deck and hastened to tumble into the pinnace. Mr. Ross, remarking that he had business at The Lost Ship Tavern, got in with dignity and took the tiller.

"Give way," he growled; and off we went.

However, when we came to where Tom Cocklyn's boats lay, and the men ceased rowing, Mr. Ross walked only to the shore end of the rotting wharf with me.

"Freckles," says he very solemnly, "when, by virtue of his commission, Governor Eden calls a Court of Vice-Admiralty to judge the prize taken by the sloop-tender *Moth*, I ought to share in a very pretty fortune. Did you guess that much?"

"You well deserve it, my lord," said I with a smile that was nearly a grin. For it annoyed him when I called him a lord, who was only youngest son to one and had no more title than fortune.

Holy angels, I know not why I was so cruelly possessed to plague this young man; but, within me, a little devil seemed to sing and caper, urging me to mischief.

"Freckles," says he, "when I am rich I shall purchase your articles of indenture from Tom Cocklyn."

"Thank you, my lord."

"And," says he, angrily, "I shall then take measure to adopt you under the law. It is high time, too!"

"Why, my lord?"

"Because you are saucy and should be properly schooled.... And otherwise controlled and instructed; and the virtues of your sex more modestly developed—"

"Oh, la, sir," said I, "would you set up a school for wayward girls aboard the *Moth*?"

"Damnation," says he, "will you not be serious? And—a little kinder, Nancy—"

"Sir," said I, "when will his lordship again bestow his noble presence and his handsome sloop upon this humble puddle called Topsail Inlet?"

He shot at me an exasperated glance: "Never, perhaps," he

muttered, "if Mr. Teach has his way with me."

That sobered me instantly, and I gazed fearfully upon him.

"I thought," said I, "that the Governor of Virginia had sent out warships to take the pirate, Teach."

"He has sent Lieutenant Maynard and two sloops. Yes. But Black-Beard has three ships and a tender. He calls himself Commodore; and his ships all fly the death's-head.... I think Sir George and Mr. Rhett and I are needed to lay this sea-wolf pack aboard."

I was so frightened that I came to him and would have taken hold of his hands, only that he took tight hold of mine.

"Nancy," says he, "under the law you belong to Tom Cocklyn," says he, "and are servant to him until redeemed," says he, "and are tap-boy in his accursed tavern yonder.

"But," says he, "you shall see happier days; and I swear it; for you are sweet and kind and good," says he, "and are valiant although a child—"

"Eighteen in November, my lord!"

"Gird at me as you please," said he; "nevertheless, I love you dearly, Nancy Topsfield."

"And I you, sir.... And, if redeemed, and by you adopted, would willingly be to you a loving daughter."

He gave me a strange, quick look of consternation, then went very red.

"You know," said I, smiling, "that I could not truly be a son to you, my lord."

He muttered something; I think it was "damnation." Which, somehow, made my heart turn tender. Then fear returned again; and I pressed his hand very fervently and begged him to have a care for himself at sea and never to conduct rashly; and to come again to Topsail Inlet as soon as might be.

So we parted; and I did not wish him to go, for a thousand terrors were beginning to take shape within my mind. But we parted—inarticulate at the end—and I bewildered and too close to tears to trust my voice.

As far as I could see his topsail and top-gallant—for his sloop carried these—I watched. When the pale sloop glimmered once or twice and melted into nothing 'twixt sky and sea, and when what I stared at proved to be a gull, I turned away toward The Lost Ship Tavern, no longer light of heart and foot; and nearer to maturity than the half-starved youngster, Nancy Topsfield, ever before had been.

As I trudged over the dunes along the sandy path fringed by bayberry and coarse grasses, I thought the weather-beaten old tavern seemed strangely lifeless.

Except for the kitchen, shutters were closed and barred over all windows on the ground floor.

I had expected to see Tom Cocklyn, with pipe and spy-glass, squatting like a great crab on the settle under the taproom window. The green settle was empty.

However, I saw a thread of smoke above the kitchen chimney, and noticed chickens pensively wandering in the garden. So I went to the side porch and, finding the door open, entered.

Moll Fair sat in the chimney corner eating ash-cake and bacon, and had a great pewter of Bath beer beside. Her hair was in a braid and her stockings off, like the pretty slattern she was; and when I came in she stared at me, her mouth full of bacon.

I asked her how she did, and she swallowed her mouthful and answered that she did well enough.

"Where is Tom Cocklyn?" I asked, seating myself.

"He's gone mad," she said.

"Gone mad! Where is he, then?"

She said she thought he was at Hangman's Point.

"Very likely," said I, "because if he were here you would not sit there with a quart of buttery beer."

She took a satisfied pull at her pewter, wiped her red mouth with her apron.

"Why do you think Tom Cocklyn has lost his senses?" I demanded.

"Well, listen," says she. "There came three ships and a tender to anchor off of Topsail Inlet while you were away at Edenton, and these were pirates and showed black colours and bloody flags and death-jacks as impudently as Sir George Sayles shows the Cross of St. George.

"I sat here where I sit now, and black Herith was a-roasting of a capon for Tom Cocklyn's dinner, and I a-dressing of it, and a slice o' bread to catch the drippings, which I love to eat—" Here she swallowed a slice o' bacon and took a pull at beer:

"So," says she, "I heard Tom Cocklyn a-cursing and a-damning on the settle under the taproom window, and I went out and there saw the three ships heading in, all showing black colours.

"'Lawks!' says I in a fright, 'here is a fleet of pirates a-sailing up our inlet,' says I.

"'The great ship,' says he, 'is *The Man-o'-War*, Captain Teach, who is called Black-Beard. And the topsail sloop,' says he, 'is *The Revenge*, and Richards is her master. And t'other sloop is *The Adventure*, and her master Israel Hands. As for the tender, I know not,' says he, 'and I wish they all were a-sailing through hell,' says he, 'and their magazines a-fire, and be damned to them!'

"And with that he fell to raging and cursing and crying out that if all the world were turning pirate he'd be cursed if he also did not go back to his old trade and hoist the bones and sail to take all nations.

"'My God,' says I, 'what has come over you?'

"'Why,' he yells at me, 'I sicken of my honesty when half the sea-captains and all the privateers that swim the seas in this hour are as great villains as Edward Teach yonder!— And so is Charles Eden, our Governor, and Mr. Knight, his secretary!' he bawls, a-tearing of his hair which is rash, for he is nearly bald, as you know, Freckles—"

"Get on with your story!" said I in a panic. "Did these sea-rogues come to an anchor and make a landing here?"

"They sailed on," said she, "but off the Dead Horse the great ship lay to and sent a boat ashore. Up they came in their shirts and red and yellow jackets, and their wide pants and naked legs in fancy boots, and bristled thick with pistols and the like.

"And there, O God! was Black-Beard, a great, hairy man with his beard tied in pig-tails and ribbons and his wild little eyes of a lunatic.

"Up he strides and takes Tom Cocklyn by the hand and, with a rotten mouth full o' curses and oaths and filth, he tells Tom Cocklyn how he loves him like a brother because he is a true man and a merry cully.

"'You lie,' says Tom Cocklyn, 'for I'm neither a true man nor a merry one! You are a great villain, Ned Teach,' says he, 'but I mean to be a greater villain than you, so help me God, for I'm sick of honesty and poverty and feeding folk in my tavern, and I mean to go to sea and teach you how it's really done!'

"At that Black-Beard let out a roar o' laughter and clapped Tom Cocklyn on the back; and all went into the taproom and fell to drinking flip.

"'Where,' says Black-Beard, 'is your tap-boy, Tom?'

"'Damn him,' says Tom Cocklyn, 'I sent him to Charlie Eden to fetch away my prize money in *The Queen Anne's Revenge* and the French sloop which was English. And the young rat tarries, and I think hath stolen the bag o' gold and run away into Virginia.'

"'By God,' says Black-Beard, 'I came here to catch him, and am sorry if he has run away.'

"'What,' says Tom Cocklyn, 'has he done you, too, an ill turn with our Governor?'

"'No,' says Teach, 'but Francis Farrington Sprigg does not love him; so I came to reckon with him on Captain Sprigg's account.'

"Well," said Moll Fair, "with that he pulls out a pair of pistols and shoots at the taproom windows and shatters the glass. That's why the shutters are closed and barred. And when Tom Cocklyn cries out on him and curses him, Black-Beard and his sea-rogues fall upon Tom Cocklyn and beat him and thrust him into the pantry. Then they take every bottle and, when they have robbed the till, off they go a-roaring with mirth and very merry to have done Tom Cocklyn so stiff a turn which they considered a huge joke.

"And, going off, when they passed near the pantry where Tom Cocklyn was bolted in, Black-Beard shouts: 'There is only one greater ass in all the world than Stede Bonnet, and this is yourself,

Tom Cocklyn!'

"And Israel Hands gives a kick upon the pantry door; and, says he, 'You take pay from rogue and pious hypocrite alike, and that will be your undoing if ever I discover you at sea, Tom Cocklyn!'

"Then Ike Ferritt, master of the fleet tender, opens the pantry door and spits upon Tom Cocklyn and tells him he has no liver in him, nor any lights nor heart nor gizzard, being a coward.

"So," said Moll, wetting her red lips with the pewter, "off they go and hoist anchor and make sail southward. And I, more dead than alive, came from the kitchen and let out Tom Cocklyn."

"And then?" I demanded, aghast at such a story.

"Why, then," said she, "Tom Cocklyn went stark, raving mad; and is still a crazed man at this hour! For, at first, all he did was to stamp and scream and yell that he must have the lights and liver out of Ike Ferritt.

"But the next day he took a dory and went into Old Clarendon, where strange folk have come since the Tuscarora war is ended in those parts.

"There he purchases a hag-boat, and ships a crew in a day, and—oh, my God!—he christens that hag-boat *The Crazy Jade*; and means to put to sea and hoist the death's-head to take all nations—"

"Tom Cocklyn," I cried, "gone pirate again?"

"Yes; and has taken black Herith, who was his old cockswain."

"Where lies this hag-boat?" I demanded.

"*The Crazy Jade?* Off of Hangman's Point."

"Holy angels," said I, "what is to become of The Lost Ship Tavern then?"

She shrugged her plump shoulders: "He bade me stay here and feed the horses, hogs, and hens until he came again with Ike Ferritt's head tied to his bowsprit."

"Certainly," said I, "Tom Cocklyn is gone mad and has no longer any understanding.

"Nevertheless," said I, "though he turn pirate and lunatic a hundredfold, he shall not say of me that I stole his money and ran away. No; for I have fetched his money from Edenton and"—I drew the bag from my shirt—"here it is. And I mean to go instantly to Hangman's Point and reckon with this wild rogue who calls me thief and runaway—though he so slanders me to the greatest wretch unhung, who is Edward Teach, called Black-Beard!"

Moll stared at me: "Get you a piece in the pantry and a jack of new ale," said she, "and let Tom Cocklyn rave as he will—"

"No; I go to Hangman's Point," said I angrily; and I went forth and slammed the side door after me, which scattered the chickens a-squawking.

I was angry. I am not given to wrath; but that Tom Cocklyn should brand me a thief and a runaway was too much. He had a loose and evil tongue—I knew that—and if he so slandered me to pirates he would do so to honest folk.

So, swinging my little sack of gold, I walked very fast across the dunes, and by the pine woods; then out across bayberry and sparkle-berry scrub until I came to the dune where a horse's skull was nailed to a dead cedar tree.

From there, sure enough, I saw a dirty old hag-boat hove to; and a pinnace on the beach below, where men were stepping a brand-new mast which had been newly cut in the woods behind me.

They were a strange and dingy company for the most, with here and yon a gaudy sash or cap; but the sun glittered on their pistols and hangers and on the gold hoops in their swarthy ears.

The dirty vessel, hove to, I could not doubt was the hag-boat, *The Crazy Jade*; and it was plain enough that she never had been cleaned since her last cargo.

I descended the dune and went toward the shallop where the men were a-stepping of the new mast; and presently recognized Tom Cocklyn, who was marching up and down the water's edge with his arms folded and his beaver uncocked and pulled down over his yellow eye.

With the green one, which was his good eye, he presently noticed me:

"Lamb's-blood and codfish guts!" he yelled at me, "have you not run away, then?"

I was enraged, but I held my tongue until I came close to him.

"No," said I, "I am neither a runaway, to cheat you of my obligations, nor a thief who has stolen what belongs to you." And I pulled the little bag of gold from my shirt and threw it at him so that it struck a pistol in his red sash, which made him grunt.

When he picked it up and counted the minted pieces, he stuffed the bag into the bosom of his own shirt.

"Come, Freckles," said he, "I see I've wronged you; and I'll say this much, that you're an honest lad and have always so conducted. And I mean to reward you," says he, taking me by the arm with his left hand, which pinched like a crab's claw, having only the thumb and forefinger on it.

"So," said he, "you shall go aboard of me and sail along o' me in *The Crazy Jade* to take all nations; and you shall sign my articles and—"

"Turn pirate?" said I, frightened. "No, sir; that I never will do—"

"What's this?" he demanded savagely; "you won't sign my articles?"

"I never will—"

"Yes, you shall!" he yelled in a fit of fury. "Are you not my servant and indented to me for redemption?"

"Let go my arm!" I panted, struggling to free myself, but he jerked me off my feet, dragged me, kicking and striking at him, across the beach and flung me into the pinnace.

"Why, you filthy little lick-pot," he shouted, "if you won't take on along o' me I'll press you, dammy if I don't! You're going aboard *The Crazy Jade* to take all nations, so help me God! And if you budge out o' that pinnace I'll blow your freckled face through the back o' your skull—I will!"

As I picked myself up from the bottom of the pinnace he pulled a horse-pistol from his sash and cocked it. I thought he was going to shoot me; and some of his men came up to see him do it. But he only cursed me and, folding his arms, kept his pistol trained on me, and bade his men have done with the mast and row him back to *The Crazy Jade.*

Rage and terror combined to keep me dumb. I dared not stir a finger lest flame spurt from that black muzzle aimed straight between my eyes.

So they shipped their mast and sail, shoved off, and manned the sweeps; and Tom Cocklyn floundered aboard, and away they pulled.

So frightened was I because of this horror which so suddenly had overtaken me that all my strength and courage collapsed. I was so weak that I could scarce clamber aboard *The Crazy Jade* when we came alongside her.

On deck, Tom Cocklyn gave me a kick which sent me spinning forward toward the forecastle, where somebody kicked me aft again, so that I stumbled against a gun and held to it.

But nobody offered me any further incivilities, for they were hoisting in the pinnace and getting the hag-boat under way.

My body hurt where I had been kicked, and I stood rubbing the bruises and staring about me at this horrible hag-boat upon which I was a prisoner and was like to perish before done with it.

Like most pirate vessels, she had been cut away and cleared fore and aft; and there was now no quarter-deck but only a poop and a forecastle; and the waist all cleared for a gun-deck.

Yet, beside the pinnace she carried a cock-boat and a skiff; and when the lousy crew mustered forward I saw that black Herith was cockswain, one Crawlin, skiff-swain, and a certain hairy old man, Jake Wolfort, boatswain. The mate was named Dane, and seemed stupid but not brutal.

The hag-boat was brig-rigged, but all her rigging, hamper, spars, sails, stays, shrouds, bitts, and planking looked rotten. Her guns, too, were battered and rusted; and carried no tomkins, only a truss o' straw to plug 'em, and a ragged tarpaulin or two for jackets. They were carronades and thirty-two-pounders.

She steered by whip-staff; I noticed that when she was under way and wallowing out through Dead Horse Inlet.

When, finally, something of calm and self-control returned to me, I limped over to the quartermaster, Mr. Shere, and asked him where I was to mess and bunk and to which watch assigned.

But Tom Cocklyn, on the poop, bawled at me to go to his cabin and await his pleasure. Which I did; and sat down there by the captain's table in such fear and misery as I had never known since the loss of my father's ship.

I set my elbows on the table and took my face between my hands. Then I noticed that there was spread upon the table, under my very nose, a black flag with the death's-head on it; and, at the mere sight, I trembled violently and hot tears ran over my quivering face.

At that instant Tom Cocklyn came in; and when I saw him I wept aloud.

"What are you about," I sobbed, "who have accepted of the King's pardon and every benefit of his proclamation? What has possessed you suddenly to fly the death's-head and sail in this vile hag-boat to take all nations?"

He seemed somewhat taken aback by my grief and what I said to him. Then he gave me a wild look, and, says he:

"You are right, for I shall take all flags, even a black or a bloody one; and if I can lay Ike Ferritt aboard who hath spat upon me, then he shall hang from my mizzen."

"You are mad," said I through my gulps and tears; "go back to your till and taproom, and to your hens and your hogs! For if Sir George Sayles sight you he will blow you out of the water! And if Mr. Ross notice you, he will surely overhaul you and you shall hang and sun-dry on Eden sands, so help me God!"

"You snivelling swipe," says he scornfully, "you pious lick-spit, have you no heart to seek your fortune?"

"None to seek it under the black flag, and my very bones turn to water at the thought—"

The loud racket of a drum beaten on deck drowned my voice. Tom Cocklyn ran to the door, and I followed him on deck, where we saw our drummer beating the alarm and marching up and down while the mate's hoarse voice called to quarters and the dirty deck swarmed with men.

Again our mast-head hailed as Tom Cocklyn reached the poop. There was a stiff north-east wind blowing, and we carried a vast mass of dirty sail; but Cocklyn shouted to Mr. Dane to clap on every stitch, and ran to the bittacle, where were two compasses and a light between them, also a sand-glass.

Mr. Shere, our quartermaster, had the helm.

Now, through the rolling of the drum, I heard the gunner shouting to the gun-crews; but there was no order or discipline aboard and only such old men-o'-war's men, or former pirates, knew what to do.

I saw the master of arms and the gunner's mate serving out cutlasses and muskets and pikes; I saw the ports triced up; guns cleared and run out, and matches lighted; but I had seen nothing of any other ship except our own.

We were running before the wind, south-southwest, and a heavy cross-sea bumped us till I could almost feel the rotten hulk shaking loose from every timber. All the while the wind-blown voice from aloft was setting Tom Cocklyn frantic; and he screamed and yelled his orders till I thought his gullet must rip apart.

Suddenly I saw our chase—first her topsail, over the seaward dunes in the sound; then, very soon, hull, spar, and sail as she headed out the inlet where we were racing to bottle her and take her. She was a sloop and carried a vast cloud of canvas white as snow.

Tom Cocklyn ran screeching about the poop, and I never shall know what he yelled, so thick flew his curses; but I saw our black flag hoisted and streaming wildly, showing the bones and death's-head to the stranger. Instantly our fore-port thirty-two exploded, banking our bows in smoke.

Now, straining my eyes to see what our chase might do, what was my amazement to discover that another sloop was chasing her, and was coming out of the inlet and showing a black ensign like our own.

At the sight of another sea-rogue, Tom Cocklyn went stark mad, cursing, bellowing, and shouting that it was Ike Ferritt in his sloop-tender a-chasing of our proper quarry.

If Ferritt guessed who we were I know not; but, when Tom Cocklyn seized the helm and bore down on him, Ike Ferritt tacked, sheering off to avoid us, but so close to the bar was he that he could not escape us; and grounded the next moment.

As we ran by him we gave him our starboard broadside, then our after guns; then, tacking, came alongside with only the inlet width between us, and gave him our larboard battery so that his deck went up in splinters.

Down crashed his mast, carrying with it everything aloft. We hove to and lay abeam, cannonading him where he heeled helplessly to leeward, her starboard guns under, and our shot tearing him to the keel.

Now came to us the piteous howling of Ferritt's sea-rogues; and I saw Ike Ferritt mount his taffrail and bawl to us that he had struck and asked only for good quarters.

Then Tom Cocklyn took a musket and hailed Ferritt from the poop.

"You spat your spittle upon me," he shouted, "but I spit lead; and how do you like it, Ike?"

Then he fired upon Ferritt, who let go the rail and rolled down the inclining deck, jerking and twitching and squealing like a crippled rat; and there he lay in the scuppers, striving to get up.

Then Tom Cocklyn, roaring with laughter, vowed he'd have sport with him; and ran to a carronade and laid it himself.

"Ike!" he cried, "turn your head and look upon me to see what I am a-doing of!"

I saw the dying pirate turn his head and look into the black muzzle of the carronade. As he shrieked, Tom Cocklyn fired; and the air was filled with fragments of men and ship, which even spattered aboard us, so near we lay.

Now Ferritt's sloop was all afire, and nobody alive aboard save only here and there a poor, wounded wretch calling pitifully to us for quarters. Cocklyn shot two of these and, as the fire spread and burned hotter, left the others to roast alive; and very soon we were in full chase of the other sloop, crowding her ever landward and hedging, and bearing down on her, so that at last she bore away on a starboard tack. We thought she meant to drive ashore; and we fired our bow-gun at her and then our starboard battery.

But no; there was a creek hidden by high dunes and into this she flew and was gone from view in a trice, while we fired upon her with our stern chaser.

After her tumbled *The Crazy Jade*, our blood-maddened crew howling and cheering, and Tom Cocklyn gone to mast-head to spy out what he might view.

Oh, Lord, he discovered a-plenty inside the sound; and near fell to the deck with fright and astonishment. For before he could give an order I saw a topsail and St. George's cross a-whipping in the wind above the dunes; and out upon us like a falcon rushed a station-ship of the Royal Navy—a topsail schooner—which swooped upon us with her bow-guns roaring and every swivel and musket aboard sweeping *The Crazy Jade*, bow, stern, waist, from forecastle to poop.

I heard Mr. Dane call out that a shot had smashed our stern-post and he could not steer.

Tom Cocklyn rushed aft and began to shove and jerk the whip-staff, but to no purpose; and he seemed in a panic of sudden fright.

Now the King's ship gave us her larboard guns all together—oh, God, what an uproar!—and our rotten timbers and standing rigging collapsed. Down crashed fore and mizzen top-masts, carrying away yards and stays and a frightful confusion of wreckage. Another blast, and our starboard battery was smashed, dismounted, scattered; our mizzen-mast, cut through, fell upon the poop and crushed it and the round house whither I was attempting to creep away to hide me in the cabin.

Then Tom Cocklyn turned sheer coward. I saw him dragging his drummer-lad to the poop to beat a parley and crying out all the while that he had struck and for Mr. Shere to strike his colours.

A musket ball hit the drummer, and he and his drum fell from the poop and went a-rolling through an open gun-port into the sea a-splash!

Mr. Dane snatched a cutlass and severed the halyards so that the death's-head fell just as a broadside from the King's ship enveloped us with flame and smoke and shook our hull into a floating ruin.

Through the stifling obscurity I saw the schooner lay us aboard; and her men come leaping over our rail where our dead and wounded sprawled, and where our scared rogues stood trembling and empty-handed, and all a-roaring lustily for good quarters.

We had made a shameful fight of it, and I think the station-ship held us in deep contempt, for her people did us no violence, but took our weapons and drove us below with kicks and jeers.

And thus it was that I was taken in piracy aboard a known pirate, and under black colours, and by a King's ship. And, for all I knew, must hang with the others who could hope for no other fate. For there was no escaping the gallows save only a death-release by their own hand; and all knew it. But not one laid hands upon himself to escape the death of shame reserved.

It was horrible below hatches; and a frightful stillness among these wretches.

From the deck we could hear a great trampling; noises of axe and hammer where they were clearing away wreckage and patching up so that we should not sink where we lay rudderless.

For, despite her battering, the hag-boat, *The Crazy Jade*, still swam like a doused witch, and it seemed a miracle that plank and timber held.

Nobody came near us. We had no food, no water. In darkness the hours dragged on. Finally I slept. But what time passed I could not know or guess when I awoke; and only knew that I was perishing of thirst and that *The Crazy Jade* was in motion—no doubt in tow of her conqueror, or, perhaps, with jury mast and trysail, floundering toward port with a prize crew on deck.

On the second day they opened the hatches and lowered water to us and a sack of hard bread. On the third day we came to an anchor.

When the hatches were removed they summoned us; and we shambled forth, filthy, starving, blinking like foul night-birds surprised by daylight.

As I climbed wearily to the deck and set foot upon it, somebody took hold of my arm and pulled me aside. I peered at him out of sun-blinded eyes, but could not see clearly, or know him until I heard his voice:

"Are you not my young friend Freckles, of Edenton?"

"Oh, heavenly angels," I whimpered, "is it Colonel Rhett who speaks to me?"

And now, clearing my eyes with trembling hands, I saw that he was Colonel Rhett who gazed at me very strangely, still holding to my arm. But suddenly I forgot I was in danger of hanging, but remembered only what a filthy and squalid figure I cut under the eyes of this elegant young man. And, less from fear and grief than from sheer vexation, woman-like I hid my face in my dirty hands and began to cry.

"Rhett!" came a gay voice that startled me, "shove that lad into line to go ashore!"

I dropped my hands and gazed up at the poop-deck, out of streaming eyes, upon a face and form I never forgot awake, or in my dreams.

"Mr. Ross!" I sobbed.

He started as though shot at, caught my eye, sprang down the stairs, and took hold of both my hands.

"Tom Cocklyn pressed me for *The Crazy Jade*," I wailed, "and we were in battle with Ike Ferritt, who had spat upon Tom Cocklyn, and we sank him, and chased a sloop; and so were taken by a King's ship—and—ooh—h!" I sobbed, "I am like to hang for it on Eden Sands—"

Mr. Ross gathered me into his arms and gave Mr. Rhett a strange, yet hardy, look.

Then, holding me, he kissed my soiled face and cast another look at Mr. Rhett, who seemed astonished. I peered fearfully from one to the other. Suddenly Mr. Ross blushed.

"My God," said Mr. Rhett, "is *that* the case?" He gave me an amazed glance; then he also reddened. "I might have guessed," said he.

Then he came close to me, smiling that charming smile I knew.

"You are too pretty for a boy," said he; "I might have known that day in Edenton when we rode the same horse together—"

He looked impudently at Mr. Ross: "And I wish I *had* known," said he. Then, laughing at me: "Prisoner," says he, "fall out for special punishment.... Mr. Ross, take your prisoner.... And God have mercy on you both!"

CHAPTER VIII
THE GOLDEN MOON

Although both Mr. Ross and Colonel Rhett knew I was a girl and no boy, and that I was not a pirate but had been pressed, I now found myself in a sorry pickle.

For I had been taken in piracy aboard that filthy snow-rigged brig and hag-boat, *The Crazy Jade*, Tom Cocklyn her master, and known as an old pirate.

And it was Colonel Rhett who laid us aboard in his sloop *Sea Nymph*, Captain Farier-Hall, carrying eight guns and seventy men, and being then, together with her consort, in search of the pirate Stede Bonnet—that great fool who knew not the stem from the stern of a cockle-shell.

Oh, heaven, what a dish of fish! And so innocent was I that I did not even know we had been made prisoners near the mouth of the Cape Fear River; for I had been driven with the others, at the point of Rhett's pistols, below deck; and thus towed to Charles-Town under hatches, and there delivered aboard the *Moth*, sloop-tender to the station-ship, Lieutenant Ross commanding.

Had it not been for Colonel Rhett's knowledge of me in Edenton, and that Mr. Ross was my firm friend, I must have suffered on the gallows like any other sea-rogue. Both of these gentlemen were tender and kind to me; both waited upon Governor Johnson in my behalf.

Nevertheless, law is law in South Carolina, if not in North Carolina; Black-Beard, with three ships flying the black flag, had grossly insulted Charles-Town and laid it under tribute; and Vane and his company of sea-devils had behaved as impudently.

So I was obliged to face a court of justice with Tom Cocklyn and his officers and crew of *The Crazy Jade*. Because only a jury could find me innocent for the law to free me. Also, the King's Majesty was like to use me as an evidence; and I must plead.

There being no public prison in Charles-Town, Tom Cocklyn and his rogues were committed into custody of the Provost Marshal and his men at the watch-house; but I was delivered into the Marshal's custody at his own residence, and wore no irons but was used with civility.

On the 28th of October, Robert Johnson, Esqre, Governor of South Carolina, called a Court of Vice-Admiralty in Charles-Town.

That day came to see me the captains of his Majesty's station-ships, *Pearl* and *Lime* and *Scarborough*, to do me a service, if possible, by testimony concerning Governor Eden's knowledge of me. But Mr. Ross feared that such testimony might injure me because of suspicions regarding the Honourable Mr. Eden and his suspected commerce with certain pirates to his own and shameful profit. However, Mr. Robert Maynard, first lieutenant of the *Pearl*, was my evidence that I made a very desperate voyage by canoe to carry an alarm into Virginia regarding the pirate Black-Beard.

He was a fine gentleman, and came in a sloop-tender, and smiled very often upon me during the trial. Also, afterward, came to take my hand and call me a gallant lad.

But my quill outstrips my story; so now to the trial. The Honourable Nicholas Trott, Judge of the Vice-Admiralty and Chief Judge of Carolina, and several Assistant Judges presided.

First, the King's Commission was read, and a Grand Jury sworn, which found the bills.

The petit jury was then sworn and the master and crew of *The Crazy Jade* were arraigned; being:

> Myself
>
> Tom Cocklyn, master
>
> David Dane, mate
>
> Peter Shere, quartermaster

Also the cockswain, who was that poor, fool, black Herith; and nine foremast men—all who were left alive out of the officers and crew of that dirty hag-boat, *The Crazy Jade*.

Every rogue pleaded not guilty. So did I, who, being the first questioned among the accused, called upon Tom Cocklyn, black Herith, and Mr. Shere to be my evidences.

These, very sullen, surly, and unwilling, nevertheless admitted that I had been pressed at Hangman's Point; had signed no articles; had shared no plunder, or had taken no arms into my hands; and had done nothing to help them against Ferritt or Mr. Rhett. Tom Cocklyn added that I was a white-livered lick-spit, and ought to be hanged.

I then asked for Colonel Rhett and Mr. Ross to testify concerning my character; and these two gentlemen made it very plain to the jury that I was to be relied upon.

While they were testifying, Judge Trott, perched aloft like a huge bird o' prey, fell to scratching his beak and a-ruffling of his vermilion and black plumage; and presently, fixing his large spectacles upon me:

"Topsfield," says he, "I think you are that same saucy tap-boy at The Lost Ship, whom once I had occasion to question."

"Yes, your honour."

"Ah!" He turned and looked at one of the Assistant Judges who grinned. "I think," said Judge Trott, in a hollow voice, "you once predicted that this boy would make a very competent witness in a court of law. Your—ah—judgment is vindicated."

The others gave me friendly looks; but Judge Trott's owlish visage remained very gloomy, which frightened me.

However, they had now done with me, and I took my seat again; and a mournful silence fell upon the court.

Presently, Tom Cocklyn being called and questioned, the trial proceeded very swiftly.

His plea—like that of all his sea-rogues—was that they were very honest men who had set out to take pirates, though with no warrant or commission from anybody, that they had attacked and destroyed Ike Ferritt, and had mistaken Colonel Rhett for a rover. For which, they said, they were very sorry.

Being asked whether sea-rovers ever showed St. George's Cross at the fore, they all answered that a pirate might show any colours.

Which is true.

Asked concerning the death's-head which they themselves flew, they made answer that it was hoisted to frighten Ferritt, but instantly struck to Rhett when they knew him for a King's ship.

"Yes," said Judge Trott, "after he laid you aboard. Then you struck your death's-head."

To which they made no answer.

When black Herith was questioned he seemed so stupid and bewildered that I was moved to become his evidence and to say a word for him, that I thought he did not know what he was about when he sailed aboard the hag-boat.

But in vain; for all were found guilty excepting only myself. And yet I told them that black Herith was a very good cook.

After which Judge Trott, explaining to them in a solemn and melancholy voice the wickedness of their crimes, pronounced sentence of death upon them in a kind of hollow groan.

"And now," said he in croaking tones that made me shudder, "having discharged my duty as a Christian, to set forth to you the horrid enormity of your sins and to urge you to repent, I must accomplish my office as a Judge, which is to say to you as followeth; namely, and to wit:

"That you, Thomas Cocklyn, and you, David Dane, and you, Peter Shere, and you, black Herith, late officers and petty officers of the hag-boat, *The Crazy Jade*, pirate; together with certain mariners of your company; to wit: Will Grey, George Aldred, Sam Slavin, Timothy McDermott, Arthur Wild, Henry Cary, John Wake, James O'Rourke, and Daniel Foy, shall go from hence, to the place from whence you came, and from thence to the Place of Execution, where each and all of you shall be hanged by the neck until you are dead!"

We all were standing; and the Provost and constables instantly closed around us. So we marched off with a tinkle and clank of manacles, Tom Cocklyn cursing the Judge and jury.

At the court-house door stood the Sheriff of Berkley, who told me that a boat from the *Moth* awaited me; but first took me to his office, where I set my signature to several papers, but of what nature I know not.

From thence to the wharf, very sad because of black Herith, poor fool; and sad, even, for Tom Cocklyn who must suffer on the morrow—though he never was kind to me but always brutal and sometimes cruel. And had done murders ashore, with a butcher's cleaver; and, no doubt, other horrid acts of manslaughter upon the seas.

A canoe lay by the stairs, which carried me to the *Moth*, where Mr. Ross received me in his cabin, very tenderly.

God knows what was in this young man's mind, or in my own; for I was weeping from the joy and excitement of my acquittal; and he meant to kiss me on the mouth, I think. But he turned awkward, and went red, and seemed to alter his intention, though I would have suffered his kiss with much pleasure.

So, with our hands intertwined, we sat upon the cushioned settle in his cabin; and there he told me that he was under instant orders to sail in company of Colonel Rhett in search of Stede Bonnet, the foolish pirate. Also, he said, he hoped to discover John Rackham, called Calico Jack; and perhaps even Ned Drummond, alias Edward Thatch, alias Teach, and known terribly throughout Carolina as Black-Beard the pirate—the wickedest man in the world excepting only Ned Low and Francis Farrington Sprigg.

"Freckles," said he, "this coast swarms with pirates despite our station-ships; and there are fifteen hundred of them cruising along the coasts today between Nova Scotia and Florida. So I shall stand for the Virginia Capes and there take further orders from his Majesty's station-ships *Lime* and *Pearl*. Therefore, I cannot tell you where you and I are like to see each other again."

After a silence I asked him what I was to do.

"For one matter," said he, "I am firmly decided that you shall not sail aboard me where you are in constant danger of being killed."

He pressed my hand, and I pressed his, saying that I asked nothing better than to share his dangers, who was my dear and only friend in all the world.

Whereupon he put one arm around me, and I know not what he

meant to do had not Mr. Rhett come aboard and down into our cabin; and Mr. Ross instantly got to his feet and made pretense of pacing the floor and whistling.

"Freckles," says Colonel Rhett, "Tom Cocklyn is to be turned off betwixt high tide and low; and he asks of you a last word; and his Excellency grants it."

So Mr. Ross, Mr. Rhett and I got into our cockleshell, and so ashore, and to the watch-house where, by himself, Tom Cocklyn sat in chains, eating of a pigeon-pie; and had a quart of beer for to wash it down.

When they left me alone with him: "Freckles," says he, "if I must hang, why then, I am very like to hang; and there's an end to that."

"My God, Mr. Cocklyn," said I, "will you not have a clergyman where such are to be had in every parish of South Carolina?"

"Will a clergyman be my evidence when I stand before God 'twixt ebb and flood tomorrow?" he growled. "No," says he with an oath, "I shall show my cropped ears to God, which Captain Death cut off. And if that be no reason for taking the high seas, why then, I shall fry in hell; and there's an end to that, too!"

I began to cry, but he swore at me and bade me hold my tongue and listen.

"Freckles," says he, eating all the while, "when I am dead tomorrow, the Government of North Carolina is free to seize upon my only property which is The Lost Ship Tavern at Topsail Inlet, where, lately, you were my indentured servant and tap-boy—" He took a long pull at his beer.

"As for your articles of indenture," says he, "I know not, but think that Government takes them over, and you become indented to the Proprietary. Let that go.

"But"—and he left off eating, and his visage became darkly ferocious—"Charles Eden, who is Governor of North Carolina, is a great villain, and hath compounded with pirates to his own profit; and he has cheated me!"

He seized the wrack of a pigeon and tore it with his dirty, crooked fingers and devoured it, talking all the while:

"Damnation," he said with his mouth full, "I shall writhe in my chains where I hang a-sun-drying on Gallows Point if this same Charles Eden shall profit by my death!"

He flung the pigeon bones on the floor, wiped his loose, greasy mouth:

"Freckles," says he, "when Israel Hornygold took the *Fancy Nancy*, Captain Topsfield, there was Arab gold aboard her, to the amount of £100,000! And this treasure was taken by Captain Topsfield out of a Barbary ship which hoisted black colours and attacked him; but he carried eighteen guns and he laid her aboard. And the gold was his. Then Hornygold took the *Nancy Fancy*; and Captain Topsfield's booty became *ours*."

"His and *yours!*"

"It was a partnership."

I was so startled at hearing this villain speak my father's name and the name of his ship, the *Fancy Nancy*, aboard which he and my mother had been barbarously murdered by Israel Hornygold, that I sat as one turned into stone, staring at Tom Cocklyn.

Said he, fixing his pale greenish eye on me, the other being yellow and nearly blind: "In this hour of death I cannot endure that Carolina, which hangs me, shall profit a penny by my turning off.

"Therefore," says he, "get you to Topsail Inlet before Government seizes my Lost Ship Tavern; and this is how you shall discover the Arab gold which Captain Topsfield took out of the Barbary ship and you shall take it for your own so that Government and Charles Eden and his villain secretary, Knight, shall not share it."

He began to laugh horribly, at thought of doing these a disservice; and could scarce contrive for the horrid mirth which possessed him:

"A half-starved tap-boy!" he roared. "A thin, knock-kneed lick-spit who becomes rich over night while Government licks its empty fingers!"

He got up in his chains from the straw where he had been sitting.

"Hornygold and I hid it," said he, "but never dared move it while Charles Eden remained Governor."

He thrust his bald, dreadful head, with its mutilated ears, close to mine:

"The map," he whispered, "is scratched and writ upon a great seashell; and the shell is sunk in a cask of rum in my cellar at The Lost Ship. Count five casks from the east cellar wall, westward. The seashell is in the fifth cask—"

There came a rattle of the door behind me; it opened, and the Provost Marshal came in with Mr. Ross.

"There is a clergyman come to pray with you," said the Marshal; but Tom Cocklyn turned his back on him with a growl and sat down on his straw, saying that he'd find his own way to God or miss it.

For a moment I looked upon this doomed wretch who I never dreamed had been leagued with Israel Hornygold, the murderer of my father and mother.

Then, in silence, I went away with Mr. Ross, out into the sunshine, my small head awhirl with amazement and with tragic memories.

"Well, Nancy," he whispered in my ear, "I have arranged your affair for you."

I looked at him absently: "How so, sir?"

"His Excellency, Governor Johnson, very kindly consents to take you into his family until I return to make for you a proper provision. Are you content?"

"Yes, sir; only first I have to go to The Lost Ship at Topsail Inlet."

"If you have left certain personal effects there, yonder sloop, which is about to sail to Cape Fear, can fetch them on her return—"

"No, sir; I must go."

He looked curiously at me. "What had Tom Cocklyn to say to you, Freckles?"

"When you return," said I, "you shall hear."

"You seem very secret," said he, smiling, and taking my hands in his.

"I only seem so," said I, "but in my heart desire, always, to reveal to you my inmost thoughts."

At that his wind-tanned cheeks flushed and he pressed my hands, and I ventured to press his a little. But we said nothing; only looked down at the water-stairs' foot where his shallop waited.

"Have you money?" he asked.

"Yes."

"Shall I find you at Topsail Inlet when I return? Or here?"

"Here, I hope."

At that he turned and hailed the sloop bound for Cape Fear, which lay very near the stairs, and asked them to take me to Topsail.

She was the *Wind-Flower*, Giles Vyning her master, who called across the water to us bidding me hasten for he meant to make sail at once.

So I looked at Mr. Ross, and he at me; and, God knows how I found courage, but I put up my face to his, and he kissed my lips; and I his. Then we went down to his shallop and he set me aboard the *Wind-Flower*.

We made sail immediately; and I stood by the taffrail and watched the *Moth* as far as I could see her until she became a glimmer in the haze and went out like a spark.

Mr. Vyning, master of the *Wind-Flower*, made me useful aboard his sloop, and was a kind, mild man who traded fairly and had friends on all the plantations, and carried cotton, rice and indigo but no hag-boat cargo.

So I was well found and well fed; happy in my thoughts of Mr. Ross, whom I had come to love very dearly and innocently—not then knowing anything of that deeper feeling which turns tenderness to passion and heats mind and body with divine fire.

Moreover, my mind was still astonished by the revelations made to me by that wicked villain, Tom Cocklyn, whom they must have hanged by now.

How monstrous the destiny which had been mine, to sell myself as servant to this wretch who had been leagued with the murderers of my father and mother!

Well, it was afternoon of a fair day when the *Wind-Flower* hove to off Topsail Inlet and I bade Mr. Vyning farewell and went ashore.

Nothing seemed changed as I approached The Lost Ship Tavern by the kitchen door, and saw Moll Fair, our lazy wench, sitting on the sill, a-shelling corn for the hens.

When Moll noticed me she jumped up and ran and kissed me, and seemed very glad to see me, saying that she feared I never was coming back and that she had not laid eyes on Tom Cocklyn either.

"No, nor are like to," said I, "unless his ghost comes here."

"What! Is he dead?" says she, taking hold of my arm in a fright.

"On Gallows Point 'twixt ebb and flood."

"Hanged? Oh, my God!—"

"In chains, for sun-drying."

She wept. "What is to become of us, Freckles?"

"I know not, Molly. The tavern now belongs to Government."

"Then we have no longer either roof or bed or bread," she snivelled. "Oh, Freckles, why don't you marry me and let us go seek service in Virginia?"

I looked at the pretty slattern and was inclined to laugh, but in her tear-stained face there was real woe.

"You little fat-skinned fool," said I, "if ever I marry a wife it shall be you, and that's all I promise.... Have done a-mauling me—I shall not abandon you—so cease your sniffling and care for your hens."

I gave her a gentle shove, which made her sit down suddenly upon the door-sill, and there left her gulping, and her large, shining tears a-wetting of her nose and chin.

So to the taproom where I took a bung starter, and thence descended to the cellar, which was lighted well enough from the low, iron-barred windows.

Counting the rum casks I fixed upon the fifth one, which was on skids. Under this I set a five-gallon jug; then drove the bung so that instantly the cask began to vomit Windward Rum.

When the jug was full I corked it and set another there; and, when this was full, I set others to fill until the cask ran empty.

Now, with mallet and hatchet, I drove in the head of the cask and turned it upside down. A great flat seashell fell out. I picked it up and carried it to the light; and there upon the nacre were graven writings where all the tiny letters had been stained red and some Arabic numerals tinted blue.

The shell was nearly a foot across, smooth as a pearl, and with rainbow hues. I managed to open my shirt and hide it against my body; then went to the kitchen, where Moll squatted on the hearth a-baking of ash-cakes.

Looking up, "Kiss me," says she, "for I always have loved you, Freckles—"

"Go to the devil," said I, "but I forgive your kicks and slaps and pinches!"

"Love-pinches," says she so sweetly that I let the lie pass and sat down upon the table top.

"Who has baited here?" I inquired.

"Few guests; and would not linger because I had only hoe-cake and bacon, and sometimes an egg to offer. And nobody to care for their horses or for them. So I drew what malt and strong drink they commanded and they reckoned with me in a very vile humour and hastened on to Bath-Town."

"None stayed the night?"

"Nobody. I had no clean bed-linen."

"You lazy slattern!—"

"What with the horses, hogs, and fowl, and fending for myself, I had a-plenty," says she, "without washing bed-linen, too. Here," says she, "is a buttered ash-cake and a slice o' bacon. Which proves that I love you, Freckles!"

I took the food and ate it, swinging my legs where I sat upon the pine table. She drew two quarts of malt-brew for us, and, seated upon a stool by the fireplace, became busy with her ash-cake and bacon.

"Such is life," she sighed, her mouth full, "—here today and God knows where tomorrow.... I forgot to tell you that a fleet o' pirates hove to off Topsail bar while you have been away."

"Who?"

"One Thatch, with a monstrous frightful beard, which was tied up with ribbons in a score of pigtails—"

"What! That monster here!"

"Monster?" says she with a simper. "He did me no harm more than to toy and trifle and swear to marry me when he had time."

"Oh," said I, "did he also toy and trifle with the money in the till?"

"No," says she; "he said that Tom Cocklyn was his friend and as good a pirate as the next; and he'd be damned, said he, if ever he robbed any honest fellow who gained an honest living by robbing others.

"All he desired, said he, was to discover a certain tap-boy, servant to Tom Cocklyn. But I told him you had shipped aboard *The Crazy Jade* to take all nations; and at that he roared with laughter and swore he'd find Tom Cocklyn and also have a word or two with you, Freckles."

I sat motionless while the chill of horror and of fear possessed and sickened me. These passed in the growing heat of anger which purged me of any weakness.

Moll Fair, a-savouring of her bacon, licked her plump fingers with reminiscent gaze.

"What a company!" said she; "three ships and a tender to careen and clean—or so said Captain Richards, who was one o' them, and Captain Hands.

"So they left and went aboard their ships; and Captain Thatch, in his great ship called *The Man-o'-War*, made sail to come into Topsail Inlet, and instantly ran aground!"

"Ran aground!" I repeated, astounded.

"Hard aground on the bar, Freckles. I heard the gun he fired to leeward and ran out to the dunes, and saw the great ship aground and signalling with flags.

"Then Captain Hands' sloop, *The Adventure*, stood in to help Mr. Thatch, but ran aground herself, and there lay heeled over and a-pounding in the boiling surf—" She fell to mixing another ash-cake for herself, talking all the while:

"Then," says she, "I think they quarrelled among those four ships, for I heard shots and screaming, and through Tom Cocklyn's spare glass, from my garret window, I watched them—every day while they stayed there off Hangman's Point I watched them—"

She set her cake to bake and fell to slicing bacon:

"Two dead men were washed ashore. A boat came and buried them. For three days they stripped the grounded ships. Then on the fourth day, I saw Mr. Thatch's black ensign hoisted aboard the sloop-tender; and he sailed, leaving the two wrecked ships to pound to fragments in the surf.

"When he sailed, Mr. Richards, in *The Revenge*, made after him; and the last I saw of them they were firing upon each other far out at sea and standing to the northward under every sail."

She offered me more food, but I was no glutton; and I got off the table and ran out to see what I might spy beyond the pine woods. When, at length, I came to the seaward dunes near Hangman's Point, there, on the bar, I discovered the wrecks of two ships buried in foam, and the surges a-lashing them and surf breaking and spouting high above them where gulls whirled and clamoured.

Now, all alone 'twixt sky and sea and sand, I sat me down and drew the seashell from my bosom, and there read the graven words stained with red and blue. These were the words I read:

"Follow the shadows. The November sun is the key. Reckon by that during other months.

"At three o'clock afternoon follow the shadow of the dead pine from which a green lantern sometimes hangs. Where the tree's shadow ends, set a peg.

"At four o'clock follow the shadow cast by the peg forty paces; and set another peg.

"At sunset, measure ten paces along the direction of the shadow cast by the last peg; and set here a common or grave-digger's spade, to the depth of the blade.

"The next day, at sunrise, follow the shadow cast by the spade, and continue one hundred and six paces, and there set a peg."

That was all excepting a small map traced in blue, which seemed to show Topsail Inlet and the sound as far as Hangman's Point.

As soon as I had read what was written on the shell, I looked up at the sun, which seemed to me to indicate that it was not far from three o'clock.

Springing to my feet I ran across the bayberry and sea-grape scrub till I came to the dead pine where Tom Cocklyn's green lantern sometimes was set to signal our station-ship at sea.

The tree's shadow lay dark across the sand. Where it ended I set a stick, which I broke from a fallen branch.

Now, seated by this stick, I waited until I concluded that it was close to four o'clock; then followed the direction of the peg's shadow and set another peg at forty paces.

Here again I waited; and, at sunset, took the direction of the peg's shadow and set another peg at ten paces.

Now, there being nothing more to do until tomorrow's sunrise, I hastened back to The Lost Ship.

By candlelight I ate supper with Moll; but I was too weary to gossip and she too full fed to remain awake. So, barred the door, and each to her trundle in the attic.

Now, when I set my mind to waking, I can awaken at any hour I choose. It was not yet sunrise when I was in the pantry for a draft of milk and some ash-cake and cheese.

Then I took a spade from the stable and ran across the dunes until I came to the last peg. Here I drove the spade to the blade's depth and left it upright.

Very soon over the ocean's inky rim the sun glimmered, gleamed, and shot a white blaze across the world.

From the end of the shadow cast by the spade I measured one hundred and six paces, which led me to a most horrid spot in the woods, where was slime and some of those gray, bloated snakes which stink and deal death without a sound.

Whilst I pushed a peg into the soft muck one of these rose up, towering high out of his coil, and began to sway and display the white lining inside his gaping jaws.

So I ran back for the spade, and, returning, fetched him a clip that set him squirming.

Having severed his venomous head I made a flame with flint and tinder, set fire to a pine twig, and, with this, burned a circle in the underbrush, out of which a dozen snakes writhed, fleeing the fire.

Now I fell to digging; and at the depth of three feet in the soft, black muck, came to a sunken cask. With my spade I stove in the head of this cask, threw out the fragments, and drew from it, with both hands, using all my strength, six bags woven out of fibre and lashed with rope.

God knows why I was not greatly excited; but I think that desire for money is not with me a passion; for I seem seldom to consider it at all, and am careless of it and, I fear, somewhat thriftless, being content with next to nothing when otherwise happy.

So, my heart scarcely quickened, and that mostly with curiosity—to which feminine failing I humbly own—I managed to open these fibre sacks, one after another.

All were full of Arab gold, in bars, in grains, like coarse dust, and in shapeless lumps. There was nothing else; no gems, no jewelry; nothing but this dead weight of soft yellow gold.

And now, as I was a-kneeling there a-thinking what to do, I noticed upon the ground in front of me a shadow which seemed strangely shaped like a man. To look up carelessly over my shoulder to see what cast such a shadow was an involuntary and unalarmed movement.

Then—oh, God!—the unuttered scream died in my throat and I was near swooning; for Mr. Teach stood there on the soft sand behind me, with his small wild eyes blazing at me out of the mass of dreadful black hair covering his face.

"Well, damn my lights and liver," says he, "if here is not Tom Cocklyn's tap-boy and Tom Cocklyn's treasure! A bride, by God, and her dowry—"

He began to roar and bellow with laughter as he caught my arm and jerked me to my feet.

I had in my band a bar of gold, and I turned like a wildcat in his grasp and struck him with it on the jaw so that two teeth broke off and blood gushed, wetting his beard.

Instantly he fetched me a buffet which dashed the senses clean out of me; and that was the last I knew for a long, long while.

When I came again to consciousness I lay on a ship's deck, sore, bruised, and feeling very weak.

Memory awakened a terror that sickened me, and I lay there in such a fright that I thought I must die of it.

Men were moving about the deck on naked feet; spray came aboard and sails flapped and filled with a soft, thunderous sound; and all around me rose the clashing, slapping, foaming noises of watery waves; and the wind in stay and shroud whistled and whined aloft.

So terrified was I that I dared not move, but opened one eye a little. I was looking aft and there saw a man steering. He was dressed in scarlet cap and coat, and in white, flapping pants of flowered Chinese silk. The wind blew his long hair about his face, which was burned nearly black. Two great jewels flashed in his ears.

All about me padded the sea-wolves, more strangely and gaudily clothed than ever I had seen, and many wore jewels and fathoms of gold chains from which crosses and lockets swung.

Presently a man passed whose eye caught mine as he stepped over me. He came around to the starboard side and squatted down beside me.

"Well, my lass," says he, "you are mending. Three days since you vomited blood and I thought you were going."

At that I opened both eyes and stared at him.

"The captain gave you a beating fit only for a grown man," he growled. "I'm Jack Husk, ship's doctor, and I swear I thought you dead when they fetched you aboard *The Golden Moon!*"

"How long have I been here?" I managed to ask.

"It's ten days since you came. It's good for you that your ribs bend and don't break. Jesus, what a beating! Can you stand? Move your legs and arms."

I was sore, but I knew well enough I could stand; but did not dare.

I looked at Jack Husk. He was not an ill-looking young man, only his features seemed sottish as though reddened and swelled by drink. He had a kind voice and a swine's eyes—brown with white eye-lashes.

"What is this ship?" I whispered.

"*The Golden Moon*, sloop-tender. We are off Ocracoke and standing for the inlet to lie up and careen."

"What will Mr. Teach do to me?" My lips scarcely formed the words.

The ship's doctor scowled. "You lie snug, you poor little devil," said he, "and I'll tell him you've three ribs broken. Damnation," said he, "I'm no child-killer, if I do live a free and hardy life. No, by God, I'll do my best for you." He got up, stepped over me, and walked aft. Later he fetched me bread and broth and a cup of water flavoured with gin.

All day I lay there on deck, my head on a coil of rope, a ragged sail to cover me from the shrewd November wind; and ever I was fighting down fear and striving to consider how I might get free of these frightful men.

When we passed in Ocracoke I saw the dunes and the dark, mournful pines beyond, and a blood-red sunset behind them flooding sea and land with hell's own blaze.

When we hove to and anchored close inshore, Jack Husk came and took me in his arms to the forecastle which, he said, was a device of Mr. Teach, with two swivels pointing aft in case of mutiny.

He told me that, except for the watch, all had gone ashore to camp there and carouse before giving *The Golden Moon* her boot-tops. Already I heard pistol shots very near.

Also, Jack Husk told me that Mr. Teach was in his cabin, very drunk, and a-firing of pistols out the cabin ports; and so not likely to annoy me.

As I was all alone in the forecastle I tested my strength by standing up and walking; and found that I could move about, though weak and sore. For which I was grateful to God because I meant to go overboard and swim for it and die in the swamps sooner than face the frightful fate that Black-Beard was reserving for me.

Now, being very weak, I went to sleep, my bed a spare sail; and so slept and knew nothing more until an explosion and a shock awoke me; and I heard Mr. Teach bellowing and cursing and many voices yelling on deck.

I got to my feet and peered out fearfully from the forecastle gun-ports; and saw the pirates running hither and thither to make sail and to train the few guns that *The Golden Moon* carried.

Then, seeing Captain Black-Beard coming forward, I shrank into a corner and cowered there when he came a-bawling and storming in:

"Burst my guts and curse my eyes if I don't marry you though all your ribs be cracked in half," says he. "Get up, you yellow-haired jade," says be, "and give me a kiss," says he, "or I'll tie your body into a hangman's knot and hoist you aloft for a jack o' bones," says he.

But before he could take hold of me Mr. Morton, his gunner, and Garrat Gibbens, his boatswain, ran in and took hold of him, crying out that the sloops he saw bearing down on us were two King's war sloops, and meant to lay us aboard.

At that, Mr. Teach fell into a rage so violent that he could not speak, but only howled and stamped, and took from the bandoulière two pistols which he cocked, howling all the while. And so rushed aft. And I, on my feet instantly, ran out to the gun-deck to see. At that instant *The Golden Moon* ran aground and listed broadside to the shore, her sails and her black flag flapping drearily.

And now, close astern, I saw a sloop flying the King's colours, bearing down on us through the intricate channel, making her way under sail and oar.

Now I saw Black-Beard get up upon our taffrail to hail the King's sloop; and, to his fury, discovered another sloop coming up behind her.

"Damn you!" he yelled, "who are you?"

Then I saw an officer on the King's sloop and knew him to be Lieutenant Robert Maynard, of the *Pearl*, station-ship.

He laughed and called out to Mr. Teach: "You should know the

King's colours, I think!"

"Send your boat aboard me!" bawled Teach, "or I blow you out of the water!"

"I'll come aboard you in my sloop," replied Mr. Maynard as his vessel drew nearer.

"God rot your heart!" yelled Teach, "and damnation seize my soul if I give you any quarter, or take any!"

"I want none," replied Mr. Maynard coolly, coming to an anchor, doubtless because of shallow water.

At that *The Golden Moon* let go all her guns at the King's sloop; and, when the smoke cleared, not a soul was seen on her deck excepting Mr. Maynard, who had the helm.

Another broadside from *The Golden Moon* crippled the second King's sloop, which was *The Ranger*, and drove her ashore.

Mr. Teach's quartermaster, Tom Miller, and Owen Roberts, his carpenter, came a-running with glass bottles full of powder to serve as bombs. Into these were stuck matches.

"Blow 'em to hell!" roared Black-Beard, hurling a bottle aboard Maynard, which burst with a loud report. Then bottles flew thick and fast amid a roar and fury of flame and smoke as the two vessels drifted together.

"Lay 'em aboard!" shouted Black-Beard; "they're all knocked in the head!"

I saw him jump down on Mr. Maynard's deck, followed by a dozen or fourteen of his ruffians. Suddenly, as the smoke of the bombs cleared away, Mr. Maynard's men sprang upon his deck and fired a volley at the pirates.

Then, beneath me where I clung to the larboard rail, I witnessed the most bloody and frantic scene my eyes ever had beheld. Everywhere men were at throat-grip all over the deck, which streamed blood so that even the water around the two sloops was stained scarlet.

I saw Mr. Maynard shoot Black-Beard through the body. I saw Black-Beard shot by Mr. Maynard's men five times with as many pistols, and still he stood and only yelped as each bullet hit him;

and swung his heavy sword with the strength and ferocity of a devil out of hell.

Mr. Maynard gave him a cut with his hanger that made a horrible wound between neck and shoulder; and Black-Beard howled at him and gnashed his teeth and slashed out to shear his head from his body.

But now the sword-cuts rained on Black-Beard so that he spouted blood; yet his great body endured like an oak, though mangled by five bullets and more than a score of sword-cuts.

He had six pistols hanging to his bandoulière. Streaming and squirting blood he unhooked the last one to fire upon Mr. Maynard.

Then, as he cocked it, he let out a bull's bellow and fell down in his blood; and a man-o'-war's man struck off his head with a pole axe.

"Tie it to our bow-sprit," said Mr. Maynard, calmly looking around his deck where, now, every pirate lay dead or wounded.

Then Mr. Maynard looked up at *The Golden Moon*, and saw me, wide-eyed, regarding him.

"In God's name," said he, "are you gone a-pirating again, Master Topsfield?"

He came aboard as he spoke, and some of his men followed, and struck the black ensign and fired a shot or two down the hatch where cowered those sea-rogues who had remained aboard *The Golden Moon*.

I stood leaning wearily against the mast when Mr. Maynard noticed me again. Something about me—my attitude, my figure, perhaps, for I was less thin and boyish now—engaged his attention.

He came to me, took my shoulders and made me face him. I looked into his astonished eyes and knew he knew I was a girl. And, at that, reddened to the roots of my yellow hair.

Said he: "Perhaps you and Mr. Ross can explain this business."

"Yes, sir, we can," said I, "only, for pity's sake, get me to him, for I never wish to leave him again as long as I shall live upon this earth!"

CHAPTER IX
BONNIE ANNE

That I was born to be the plaything of Chance and the sorry jest of Fate had now become quite clear to me. It seemed strange, because always I had conducted so honestly toward all.

But here, at Ocracoke, I found myself a-wriggling again in the law's clutches, having been discovered aboard *The Golden Moon*, sloop—as I have related—which same sloop had been taken by Lieutenant Maynard's tender after a most bloody battle in the channel.

Now I had no mind to face a Court of Admiralty again when Mr. Maynard should carry his prize into port. And what price Admiralty, oh God, I knew not, but it might cost me my life.

Another matter also troubled me: *The Golden Moon* was a pirate and lawful prize to Mr. Maynard. But, stowed aboard her, was my £100,000 in bar gold, and in grains, flakes, lumps and dust, tied up in sacks woven out of reeds, which I had dug out of a marl-pit at Hangman's Point.

Of this, Edward Teach, called Black-Beard, had robbed me in the very instant of discovery. But this gold had been my father's lawful booty taken fairly at sea out of a Barbary ship; and, although Israel Hornygold and Tom Cocklyn had murdered my father and robbed him of it, nevertheless this treasure still belonged to me. And I had no mind to have my own rightful property adjudged King's booty by a Court of Admiralty, and shared between the station-ships, *Lime* and *Pearl*, together with other plunder taken by Mr. Maynard aboard the pirate, *The Golden Moon*.

Now, one might suppose that Captain Black-Beard had stored away and hidden these sacks somewhere amid his other plunder in the hold.

But mark this crafty devil's cunning, who entertained, in his secret mind, no notion of sharing my gold with his rascal officers and foremast rogues. For he had given out that there was marl in the sacks designed to barricade the bittacle against gun fire; and there lay these same sacks, all smeared thick with marl, and stacked up on the low quarter-deck to protect the bittacle from bullets! I saw them there and knew them instantly. And resolved that not even the King's Majesty should rob me of my heritage again.

Now, whilst I was pondering these matters, and seated aft upon a cable, to rest my bruised and weary body against the taffrail, I saw the beautiful Mr. Maynard come out upon the deck and gaze about him with a pleased and satisfied air. With his fine eyes and rosy cheeks I thought him too handsome for a man, and, plainly, vain of his graceful person, though as brave an officer as ever sailed.

When he saw me he came aft, carrying a paper in one hand.

"Nancy," said he complacently, "I find that I have taken near two thousand pounds' worth aboard *The Golden Moon*, and this is her inventory: eleven tierces and forty-five bags of cocoa, and twenty-five hogs-heads of sugar which, at vendue, and counting the sale of the sloop, should fetch us near three thousand pounds. And what do you think o' that, my lass?"

I said it was a snug treasure.

"More than that," said he, "I have Captain Black-Beard's papers, and letters to him from Governor Eden and Mr. Knight, which show them to be very guilty of trafficking with pirates."

I was horrified. Instantly I determined to go to Mr. Eden with this dreadful news, so that he might save himself alive if possible.

I asked Mr. Maynard, very calmly, what he meant to do with me.

"Oh," says he with a killing smile, "your pretty face and figure are sufficient evidences before any court to bewitch a jury."

"My God, sir," said I, "are you minded to send me before another Court of Admiralty! If you do, Judge Trott will surely hang me this time!"

"Were you Charles Eden, Governor of North Carolina, you might have reason for worry," said he, "for he is a rogue and you are not."

"I have reason, too, sir; and I ask you again, what is your purpose with me?"

"Why," says he, "I believe you to be innocent, and will stand your evidence—"

"Oh, Lord," said I, "who will believe that Captain Black-Beard gave me such a beating that I lay scarcely conscious for a week and more aboard *The Golden Moon?*"

"I believe it," says he with a handsome smirk, "though if you were not so pretty, Nancy, I might entertain a few doubts—"

"Hang it!" said both blushing and vexed, and dreadfully concerned regarding Mr. Eden, "what is a comely face and shape to a stuffed owl in spectacles!"

"Do you mean Judge Trott?" said he, horrified.

"Yes, I do! And his Associate Judges, too. A pretty row of birds to plead before! The Grand Jury is certain to find a bill. As for the petit jury, they are solemn gentlemen who have long since sickened of Carolina pirates, and have their bellies full; and now mean to protect their wives and children by hanging everybody. Oh, Mr. Maynard, I beg you will not send me before a court—you who know so perfectly that I am innocent of any piracy! You are a gallant man and just; but you are not so cruel as to do that!"

"What the devil would you have me do, Nancy?" says he, a-fiddling with his curled love-locks, in doubt and embarrassment.

"Let me ashore—"

"No, I can't do it."

"Well, then, turn your back whilst I manage. God—and Mr. Ross—will reward you!" I then shed a tear; which was feminine but dishonest. Instantly I noticed that he melted.

"How shall you manage?" says he, wavering. "And, for God's sake, don't weep—"

"Set me to cleaning up this dirty deck o' the battle litter. I'll heave over these marl-muddied sacks stacked against the bittacle; I'll clear away splinters; I'll swab decks and scuppers of blood. And when you go ashore, sir, to read the burial services over your dead, then I'll go too—by way of your stern cable, like a ship's rat."

His face became grave at that; he looked at his watch, at his sloop, then at me.

"Yes," says he, "I have twenty-nine dead and wounded in my two sloops—nine aboard *The Ranger*.... Very well," says he, "I shall not lock you below hatches with Black-Beard's rogues.... Well, then, heave over all this wrack.... And fetch a mop.... And, hereafter, steer wider of all sea-mischief, Nancy Topsfield."

He smiled, then smirked and patted my cheek; and, with his own handkerchief, wiped away my tears; and I know not what else he might have done; but I said:

"Have a care, sir! Would you wish your crew to see you a-kissing of a cabin-boy?"

At which he seemed startled and took himself off; and so over the side into his own sloop.

Now, it being flood tide, the stern of *The Golden Moon*, warped close inshore among the mangroves, overhung a bushy shore.

So, one by one, I seized the marl-smeared sacks of gold and dropped them over the taffrail. Some crashed into the sweet-bay and sparkle-berry bushes; others splashed in the mud amidst the mangroves and reeds.

This business finished, I ran, limping, to the forecastle and there found a mop and pail; and fell to sluicing and swabbing where the thickest blood was smeared, and it nearly sickened me to sweep up a man's severed hand and a piece of skull with hair on it.

All debris I flung overboard; the man-o'-war sentry, squatted on the hatch, smoking his pipe and watching me, and yawning now and then.

"Work," says he, "is a damned good thing, but a dry one. It's medicine for boys but pizin for such as me.... What I need," says he, "is a tot o' Santa Cruz; I do. It ain't much to ask for a honest foremast man what's fit and bled and died for his King."

Now, I had noticed a jug in the bittacle. I ran to pull the tarry stopper and sniff it. It was pineapple rum out of Barbados, and very mellow.

First I took a good look across the rail at Mr. Maynard's sloop where the drummer was now come on deck and was a-beating of his drum while the ship's bell was a-striking slowly for the funeral.

Over the gangway laid to the shore the crew were carrying their dead to bury them among the dark pines beyond the landing. And now I heard *The Ranger's* bell, also, tolling for her own dead.

Nobody noticed *The Golden Moon*, where I stood by the bittacle, and the sentry sprawled on the fore hatch. So I carried the jug of rum to the sentry, who clacked his lips and tongue in astonishment and delight; and, laying aside his musket, took the jug between both hands.

He sat facing forward, and never noticed that I took his gun and sped aft where I knocked out the flint and hid it in the bittacle.

Then over the stern I went, and slid down the cable which had been made fast to a pine tree.

Among the pines was a hospital tent to which wounded had been carried from aboard *The Ranger*, and Mr. Maynard, though now they were again aboard both sloops. In this tent I discovered a sack of hard bread, a cheese, a bag of prunes, a clean new blanket, flint, tinder, and a knife; all which I took; and did not regard it as stealing to obtain these means for sustaining life.

And then I committed a real theft—God pardon me—but was resolved that Mr. Eden should have a chance for his life. For Law is cruel.

So, seeing *The Ranger's* canoe afloat inshore below where her skiff-swain had landed her dead, I ran to it and found oars, mast, sail, and a cask of water stowed aboard.

Now I hastened into the candleberry bushes; and, one by one, carried the marl-smeared, reeded sacks of gold aboard the canoe, fishing out of the mud and mangroves the last few sacks and missing none at all.

From where I stood by the stepped mast aboard the canoe I could see Mr. Teach's severed and bloody head tied by the long, coarse, black hair to the bow of Mr. Maynard's sloop; and his long beard tied up with ribbons. And now heard Mr. Maynard's rich, agreeable voice among the pines, solemnly reading the services for his dead.

There was no time to linger. I cast off, pushed free with an oar, made sail as quietly as I could, and stood for the open sea.

For more than a mile the dunes and dark forests hid my little sail from Mr. Maynard's mast-head; and I was far on my way and bowling along just inside the sparkling inlet before I heard a distant gun; and so knew that my flight in the canoe was now discovered.

But, except in small boats, they could not give chase. It would require hours for the two sloops and *The Golden Moon*, prize, to weigh and make sail, or row out through that tortuous channel, although it was flood tide, too.

So on I sped under lateen sail; and ever a-hedging seaward out from a lee shore until I, tacking, stood away fair, before a fair wind, to the southward, a-making for Currituck Inlet with all my might and main.

Two sails I saw at sea, but they did not discover me, or, at least, took no notice.

The wind held fresh and fair out of a north-west November sky as mild and blue as June; and only for the vast rafts of wild duck and snow geese did it seem like early winter in Virginia and Carolina.

Now, had it not been for Mr. Eden's peril, I would have stood for Cape Fear to find the *Sea-Hawk*, station-ship; and carried my treasure aboard Sir George Sayles so that this most upright man should counsel me and be my confidant and judge.

But what was my gold to a human life? All my heart went out to this unhappy gentleman who had been tempted and who yielded. But I knew him to be good and kind and truly repentant; and that he had lived in cruellest fear, threatened and mocked and bullied and blackmailed by the ruffian Teach and by Tom Cocklyn.

Now that these rogues were dead it seemed hard that Mr. Eden's guilt should be discovered among Black-Beard's papers. And I meant that he should know of this before surprised and arrested, so that he might have time to take such measures for safety as he thought proper.

All that day I sailed; and part of the night, under the high silver lamp of the Rogue's Moon which made a magic of sea and land so wonderful that God alone could have wrought it.

I slept ashore under an island set with vast, black pines. Dawn found me gnawing a crust and a bit of cheese; and, chewing a prune, I set my sail and bore away to the southward, almost deafened by the rushing roar of millions of wings overhead where the wild duck, geese and swans were sweeping seaward on their morning flight.

All day long the wind held steady out of an azure sky; the great blue sound was all frosted with wave crests, where white-crested pirate-eagles soared and flapped and robbed the fish-hawks of their finny prey.

The sun went down in a lake of palest gilt; the Rogue's Moon rode red, then rosy, then turned to a disk of burnished silver ere I put in to a cove where were pines to shelter me.

Here I shipped mast, furled sail, made all fast, and went ashore, meaning to build me a fire to toast cheese and stew a few prunes to stay me.

To my surprise I discovered a road running through the woods, and, following it inland a little way, noticed some lights very near.

As I did not know just where I was, and desiring to inquire, I walked toward the nearest light; and presently saw that I had come to a little settlement where candles burned in the windows of a dozen or more log houses.

Of these, one was a tavern where a lighted lantern swung below a painted sign. It was called The Sea Horse; and there was a horse painted with a fish's tail in place of two hind legs, and fins on his forefeet; and upon his back rode a young lady wearing no garments of any description—not even a decent shift.

I knocked at the door. Nobody came; so I opened it and walked in.

As there was a chill in the air and a white fog rising, I was glad to find a fire blazing upon the hearth.

At a rough table two men were throwing dice. They had rings in their ears and wore gaudy scarfs of silk around their loose, long hair.

On a settle by the fire sat a very young girl with one leg cocked up over the side, and swinging her small foot upon which a shoe of scarlet morocco hung upon the toe. She was smoking a long clay pipe, and had a jack of ale at her elbow.

The two dice throwers looked up at me; the girl looked around at me over her shoulder. Instantly I concluded to ask no questions that might reveal me as a traveller astray and lost to reckoning, but to carry all as though familiar with my whereabouts.

A large, soft, silent man in lamb's wool slippers, waistcoat and apron, came in carrying a smoking dish of fish.

I asked him if he were the landlord and he said he was. Then I bade a good evening to the company and sat me down by the fire upon the settle, opposite to where the young girl lounged with pipe and jack.

"Do you bait here?" inquired the landlord, considering me out of two sly eyes so pale that they seemed almost white.

"No," said I, "but I could do with a dish o' fish and a pint of beer before I pass on my way home."

"Young sir," said he, "will you be good enough to name yourself?"

"Topsfield's my name," said I, carelessly, "and have taken over Tom Cocklyn's tavern, The Lost Ship, at Topsail Inlet."

Whereupon all four looked intently at me.

Then the young girl, who was very pretty, smiled. "So that's your trade, Mr. Topsfield," says she, "and you keep an ordinary."

"That's my trade; and the ordinary keeps *me*."

"Do you come now from Topsail?"

"From Virginia, homeward, and much fatigued."

"On what business?" she asked.

"My own, my lass; and am sorry it does not concern so pretty a girl as you."

She laughed. "A-wenching it," said she, "I warrant you!—a handsome young spark like you. Fie, Mr. Topsfield; you seem very young and innocent who keep so notorious an inn as The Lost Ship!"

"Is it notorious?"

Whereat all three grinned; the two rough fellows returned to their dice; the girl took a pull at her jack, another at her pipe, threw back her head and blew ring after ring of smoke toward the blackened ceiling.

The landlord, who seemed to have no servants, fetched me my beer, a dish of fish, and a bench for a table. Then, raking an ash-cake from the hearth, he set it before me and went to the till, where I could see his round, soft face and pallid eyes watching me through the wooden lattice.

When I had satisfied my hunger and was lifting my jack to take a pull, my eyes encountered the pretty girl's, which were a bright and brilliant blue and full of merry guile.

She wore her brown hair as they wear it in Holland, that is, trimmed to her sunburned neck. She wore no stays; a loose, full-sleeved white shirt, open at the throat, revealed more of her than seemed modest. Over her shirt she was clothed in a kind of sleeveless Barbary vest of scarlet stuff, stiff with silver; a scarlet sash of extraordinary width constrained her slim body from her breasts to her hips, and in it was a Barbary dagger and the longest and most elegant silver pistol I ever beheld.

As for her skirts, they were like those worn by Scotchmen, but made out of white cloth full of pleats, and were so shamefully short that her sunburned legs were bare from the knees to the tops of her small boots, which were soft, scarlet morocco.

Now, from the instant I had noticed the red handkerchief binding her temples, and the great hoops of green jade in her ears, and the hardy manner with which she drank and smoked and sprawled at her ease to confront the world, I had concluded that here was one of those impudent consorts of sea-rogues who had seen Madagascar and the dominions of the Grand Mogul in her brief span of years.

When I chanced to encounter her eyes, she smiled upon me and, from her lips, blew at me delicate, wavering rings of smoke.

"Which," says she, "are the ghosts of all those wedding rings I should have worn, Mr. Topsfield. Have you a lady-love?"

"Is it not likely," said I, "if, as you say, I have been a-wenching in Virginia?"

She laughed, lounging at her ease, her foot ever a-swinging.

Through the grille the landlord asked me what was the best news out of Williamsburg.

"Hard times," said I, "but the Tuscaroras are gone north to join the Iroquois and live among them."

"How's Spotty?" inquired the girl in her gay and impudent way.

She meant Governor Spottswood.

"Dangerous," said I, "for he hath commissioned two sloops to take that worthy mariner, Mr. Teach, and he has been taken, and his head hangs at the bows of a King's ship."

"Is that sure?" demanded the landlord.

"It is common gossip in Virginia, I believe."

One of the dice throwers began to curse and damn very horridly, saying that the times were unfortunate for men of heart and courage; that Stede Bonnet was gone and now Teach; and not only had Tom Cocklyn been taken and hanged, but Jack Rackham, also, now dangled a-sun-drying at Port Royal or thereabouts.

The girl said coolly: "No; Jack was hanged at Gallows Point, but he sun-cures at Plumb Point; and George Featherston at Bush Key, and poor Dick Corner shrivels up in his chains upon Gun Key, where the blue crabs strive all day and all night to climb the gallows to get at him."

Said I: "You seem to know a great deal about Calico Jack and his fate."

"I ought to," said she; "I'm Anne Bonny."

"Yes," said one of the dicers, turning savagely, "and that's what a man gets who loves a mistress—not a tear in his memory when he hangs!"

The girl, who was not more than seventeen at most, shrugged her shoulders:

"When my man turns coward," said she, "he no longer concerns me and there is no tenderness in my heart for him. When I love a man I love mostly his courage."

"You lie, you little Jezebel," growled the other, "you love his money best of all—"

Anne Bonny whipped her clay pipe from her lips and hurled it at him; and it hit the table and scattered burning tobacco over both men.

Both got up with savage oaths, but Anne laughed and pulled her pistol and cocked it.

"Landlord," says she, in a voice which was like a giggle, "fetch me a fresh pipe and tobacco and a coal to light it."

Growling, shuffling, cursing, the dicers resumed their seats.

"Ha-ha!" said Anne to me, "yonder sit two of Jack Rackham's company. Do you wonder that Captain Barnet took us with scarce a shot? No, by God!—down falls our black ensign and all scuttle like rats under hatches; so that I could not shame these poltroons to keep the deck and fight Barnet."

She began to laugh again, and told me she had been so angry that she fired her pistol down the hatchway where Calico Jack and his crew cowered in panic.

"Damn them all for rats," said she, "who would not defend their lives, which even a rat will do. God knows why the court acquitted Pedro Nunez yonder, and Noah Sproat."

"How came *you* free?" I asked, astonished.

"Why, Sir Nicholas Laws called a Vice-Admiralty and the jury found us all guilty. But I told them I was going to have a baby"— she burst into peals of laughter—"and they believed me! So they took me from the jail to the hospital, whence I walked out and aboard a pettiauger about to sail. And here I am"—she gave me a hardy look—"with no ship, no money, no lover.... Do you think, Mr. Topsfield, you could help me mend my fortune?"

At that the innkeeper, speaking softly from the till: "Are you so fickle, Anne, that you are done with me who have fed and clothed you since you landed in Carolina?"

"Done with you?" says she, merrily, "why, you old fat-rump, I have not even begun with you!"

"What!" says he, "have you not been—"

"Never!" says she with an impudent giggle. "You are too old and fat to please me," says she, "but here is a pretty fellow whom I already love and who can have me for a wink of his gray eye!"

"You heartless cat," growled one of the dicers, "you love with a giggle, and when you do murder you giggle, too! *I* could tell yonder lad how you used Jack Rackham the day they hanged him!"

"And how was that?" says she defiantly.

"Why, poor Jack begged to bid you farewell, and all you said was: 'If you'd fought like a man you'd not be hanged like a dog.'"

"Well," says she, "was it not the truth?"

"Was it for you to taunt him who had been his drab?"

"I'll drab *you!*" she said wrathfully, a-pulling at her pistol again; but:

"Wait a bit!" says the landlord in his soft, fat voice; and there was his pistol pointing at her through the spindles; and we all heard him cock it.

"A filthy tavern full o' cutthroats," says she with a shrug, "and I'm done with it if this handsome young man will give me a roof and a crust and a kiss every Sunday after church."

This shameless hussy, for all her youth and good looks, began to sicken me; and her bold manner and heartless ways hardened and chilled me: for she now got up and came over to my settle and sat too near me, and with bold design, a-toying with my hand.

"Come," says she, "you have sailed in the Red Sea Trade, have you not?"

"I have seen some few disputes on the high seas," said I.

"Ha! I knew you had sailed On The Account! … Do you know that I find you a pretty fellow?"

"As for that," said "I have no inclination—"

"Why? We both are young. You are a man of heart, I hope—"

"None at all."

But she only giggled and caught me by the neck and kissed my mouth so that I was near strangled and sickened with her ardour, and gave her a hearty push.

"Hang me for a sea-rogue!" said I in a passion, "if I let any wench on earth lay me aboard! Give over, I tell you; and keep your hardy hands and lips for the man who wants 'em!"

The girl flushed and there was a swift blaze in her eyes.

"Damnation," said she, "must I woo a man, then, to have him, who am accustomed to fight off men who pester me?"

But I paid her no attention and got up and, going to the till, reckoned with the landlord, pulling out the purse of gold which I had, alas, of poor Mr. Eden.

Then I said good night to him and to the company, very civilly; but Anne Bonny stopped me at the door; and when she would throw her arms about my neck I continued on, dragging her through the door with me, where I tore her loose of me in silence.

"I tell you," she cried, stamping her foot, "that I have conceived a friendship for you! Why do you treat me with contempt? Are you squeamish, Mr. Topsfield? If I am a rogue, you have been one yourself. And keep a rogue's tavern in this hour!"

I hastened on, making no answer; and the girl walked by my side, pleading sometimes, sometimes cursing and damning all men, and swearing that I should do her reason or say very plainly why I would have none of her.

"You conduct like a devil," says she, "and I know not why I endure it and shame my pride, only that I find myself possessed of a sudden tenderness for you which is a very passion—"

We had come to where I had moored my canoe. The moonlight silvered land and water all around us. When she saw my canoe she caught me by the arm and begged me to take her with me wherever I pleased.

She was not as tall as I—a small, dainty, prettily shaped girl who looked like a child and was scarcely stronger. But when I disengaged her clasp and threw her easily aside, she uttered a cry of fury, and pulled her pistol half out from the sash.

I still had hold of her; and now I struck up the silver pistol, wrenched it out of her hand, and flung it splashing into the moonlit water.

There followed a breathless and terrible silence. Then, suddenly, I boxed her ears.

That turned her to a demon, and she fell on me like a young panther, and pulled free her knife to do me a harm. But I twisted that out of her grasp, also, and sent it far out across the water to follow the pistol. And boxed her ears with all my might.

Now I had to do with a wildcat gone mad, who seized on me, tooth and claw; and there we were locked together, swaying, struggling, panting, staggering, now on the shore, now in the water, now upon the sands, again among the pines.

"You filthy pirate's trull," I gasped, "have I helped hang sea-rogues to soil myself with their sluts? Not Jack Rackham, but his dirty doxy should hang a-sunning on Gallows Point!"

At the instant, suddenly she made the discovery unavoidable in our desperate embrace; and she screamed out in rage and astonishment:

"You devil! You devil! You are no man at all, but a woman! By God, you shall pay me for this mockery—"

But I took her instantly by her swelling throat, and the cry died on her writhing lips.

In my blind anger I knew no longer what I was about, and meant to kill her; but God was merciful and stained me not with such a death. For the tall heels on her morocco boots tripped her on a tree root; we both fell, and her head hit the tree, dashing every sense out of her.

When I discovered she was only senseless and not dead, I ran to my canoe, stepped mast, hoisted sail and stood for the inlet.

There was little wind inshore, but enough outside, and flood-tide upon the bar.

So, all night long, sailed southward before the same and steady wind which had not yet failed me. And, as I sailed, still raw and bleeding from my battle, torn, bitten, scratched, and all a-tremble still, I thought of this strange youngster—so violent, so depraved, so youthful in years and so ancient in wickedness—Anne Bonny! The Bonnie Anne of ballad and broadside. The most notorious female pirate upon this earth!

And that I should lay my proper eyes on her whose lover and whose lover's ship was accustomed to keep the Caribbean, and upon whom I never dreamed I should gaze!

The sun of noon flooded the river as I carried my canoe in and hove to by the water-stairs at Edenton, where, between the tavern and the docks, were a great crowd of people standing; and I saw militia in line, leaning upon their muskets, and a troop of horse riding slowly along the street. And heard an iron bell tolling.

Then, of a sudden, looking up at the wharf where I still was seated in my small craft, I saw Mr. Rhett in his uniform and wearing his sword.

He was looking very oddly at me; and now he came down to the wharf and descended the water-stairs to step aboard me and seat himself before me.

"Nancy," says he very gravely, "what are you doing here in Edenton?"

"Sir," said I, awed by his solemn speech and features, "I am come from Virginia with a message for Governor Eden.... Why do you regard me so strangely, Mr. Rhett?"

He took my hand, held it, stroked it.

"Yours is a kind heart," said he, "both gentle and valiant. I know why you have come to Edenton; and how you came.... But two messengers have out-stripped you, my child."

"Two—"

"Two messengers seeing Charles Eden. One was Mr. Maynard, who outsailed you—"

"Oh, God!" I whispered.

"The other was a messenger more dreadful yet.... And that messenger was—Death."

I stared.

"Nancy, Charles Eden was discovered dead in his garden this morning where he sat with a book upon his knees.... The doctors say he died of fright."

Tears rushed to my eyes, blinding me.

"Yes," said Mr. Rhett, "the papers discovered in Black-Beard's cabin were fetched here by Lieutenant Maynard last night, who instantly waited upon Governor Eden and laid them before him for explanation.

"The Governor smiled and said that he could solve that mystery very easily, and would do so in the morning after he had seen his secretary, Mr. Knight.

"But this morning Mr. Knight took poison in his own home, and lies there dead of it at this hour.

"And fear slew Charles Eden, it is said, for he sits there under the trees in his pretty garden, dead in his great chair.

"And all Carolina will be in a panic when the news is known because all loved him and he was the best and kindest Governor that Carolina ever has had.... Will you come with me to the Governor's mansion to take a last farewell of one who liked you, Nancy, and had been kind to you?"

So we rose, and I took hold of Mr. Rhett's hand, who walked very swiftly along the sunny street, so that I had to run a little beside him and clasp his hand tightly, so dazed and blind was I with grief and tears.

CHAPTER X
THE SILVER OAR

Charles Eden, Governor of North Carolina, sat dead in his easy-chair under the magnolias in his garden, a book open upon his lifeless knees. A capable, kind, and gentle man. The best Governor that North Carolina yet had had.

Dead of fright!

And now I found myself in a dismal perplexity concerning my own affairs. Because there was no longer a Governor in North Carolina, I took it that there was no Government; and resolved not to trust my money there, but to carry it instantly into Charles-Town, where, God knows, there was Government both capable and severe.

Nor would I tell anybody that I possessed near £100,000 in Arab gold tied up into little bags woven out of reeds.

For I feared all Law, particularly Admiralty Law in South Carolina; and could not guess how it might use an indentured servant. All I knew was that this Arab gold had been my father's lawful spoil. That it had been foully taken from him at the cost of his life by the known pirates, Israel Hornygold and Tom Cocklyn; and concealed near Topsail Inlet; that I had discovered it; that it belonged to me, doubly now, and rightfully, and not to Mr. Maynard's crew, nor to his Majesty's station-ships in the James River.

There it lay snug in small, marl-smeared sacks aboard my canoe moored at the water-stairs. I had saved it from Mr. Teach and from Lieutenant Maynard; and now I had no intention of taking anybody whomsoever into my confidence lest some unjust law I never heard of should give my Arab gold to the King of England and his mariners.

I walked with my friend, Lieutenant Rhett, to the Eden Arms Tavern, and there he bespoke a private room, and there made me eat, and drink a glass of Madeira which heartened me; for my heart was very heavy of the tragedy of Mr. Eden.

"Nancy Topsfield," says he, "why do you still wear your boy's clothes who have no need to any longer?"

"Because," said I, "a lonely boy has more security in this world than a girl. It is true that I am given a few kicks, but none suspects my sex, and I do very well."

"Yes," said he, "but Lieutenant Ross means to adopt you when he returns from the sea."

"I am not sure," said I, blushing, "that it would suit me to be adopted by anybody."

"Do you know," said he, "that a Court of Vice-Admiralty has made Mr. Ross a wealthy man?"

I told him I was at ease to hear it; but said never a word about my own newly found fortune. My business was my own, and not Mr. Rhett's.

"I should suppose," said he, "that you had had enough of vagabonding and would be glad of a surcease from all roving."

I had had more than enough of it, but did not choose to tell him so, and only replied that, so far, I had kept body and soul united, and preferred freedom to shift for myself rather than be adopted and beholden to anybody.

The wine mellowed him, I think, and loosened his tongue somewhat; for presently he told me that I made a pretty boy and was like to make a prettier girl when properly dressed as one, and that no doubt Mr. Ross thought so too, for he seemed very fond of me.

"Also," said he, "you are close to an age, Nancy, where you are like to learn something of love. And I envy the man who first teaches you. Have you made any choice of a teacher yet?"

I turned sulky at that and made him no answer, for it was plain he thought me handsome; but my mind was too full of Mr. Ross to notice other men with kindness.

Yet, Mr. Rhett was agreeable and elegant and had a kind of reckless charm about him where he lounged on his chair, a-squinting at his brimming wine glass which he held up in the sunshine. And a-cracking walnuts now and then.

"I'll tell you this much," said I, "if I were truly at heart the vagabond gypsy I seem, then, no doubt, I am at an age—or nearly—when I might take a sweetheart where I found him.

"But, though misfortune hath made of me an orphan and an indentured servant, nevertheless I was born daughter to Captain Topsfield of the *Fancy Nancy* and am the kind of woman a man has to church if he would possess me."

"Yes," said he, soberly, "and if *you* possessed a *fortune* you might marry even a gentleman, because you are a very, very pretty creature, Nancy Topsfield."

"Though mouse-poor," said I, "only a marriage ring buys me. And if any gentleman thinks otherwise, though it broke my heart I'd send him to hell to light his candle."

"A gentleman," he explained with kindly patience, "does not marry destitute beauty in these days."

"Then," said I, "no gentleman can have any lighter traffic with this destitute beauty—if there be any such beauty as you pretend in this thin body and freckled face of mine."

"Wait," said he, laughing and filling his wine glass, "you will not always remain so ferocious, pretty one." He drained his glass and gazed at me reflectively:

"What a life," said he. "And why we all do not turn rogues like Stede Bonnet is a very mystery to me. Look at these pirates, how some among them become rich in a six-month.

"Look at Bob Culliford! He, in *The Mocha*, with his consorts, *The Pelican* and *The Soldada*, shared £300,000! Yes, and then $6,000, then $18,000, and then £400, each man, out of three Moor ships! Lord, I think I am the most virtuous man on earth not to take my own ship!"

I said that I could not eat even an ash-cake which had been stolen, for it would choke me.

"No," said he, "nor I, dammy! That's why you and I remain poor. But all honest men are not so nice as I am. No! Look at Frederick Phillips, the rich New York merchant whose great ship, *The*

Pembroke, traded with Bob Culliford and Captain Shivers—two of the damnedest pirates afloat. Well, here be I who risk life for a pitiful pay in his Majesty's Navy—and am like to risk it again very soon. Heigho! What a life!"

"Sir," said I, "do you mean to take the sea shortly?"

"Tomorrow. Why," says he with a bitter laugh, "there are today two thousand pirates ashore at New Providence pretending to await the King's pardon, but all ready to fly the bones at first opportunity.

"There are twenty-seven ships with three thousand pirates afloat off our coasts, twixt Cape Canaveral and Cape Cod!

"I do not know why his Majesty's West Indian station-ships are not more active. But all that our ships in the James can do is to send out sloops when these sea-rogues harry the Carolinas."

"Whom do you sail to take this time?" I ventured to ask.

"Why," said he, "that great fool, Stede Bonnet. I caught him a week since inside Cape Fear, and he struck his black flag to me, and I carried him and his rogues into Charles-Town for Nicholas Trott, Esquire, to hang them.

"Now comes to me a messenger saying Stede Bonnet has escaped; and I am sent to catch him again and fetch him back to be comfortably hanged."

I said nothing. I was considering how I was to get my little bags of Arab gold into Charles-Town and yet say nothing about them lest an unjust law take them from me. Yet, how was I to accomplish this with all the coasts and inlets and sounds so swarming with sea-rogues?

"You know," said Mr. Rhett, "this Stede Bonnet is a strange fellow. I think he is mad."

"Mad?" said I, absently.

"Why, yes. Otherwise, how could he turn pirate who had no need to?"

"Was he not poor?"

"Poor? No; he had a fortune. He was born a gentleman. He is a man of fine education; has been a Major in the King's Life Guards. He has a rich plantation in the West Indies, where he was respected and thought much of. He possesses wife and children, wealth and friends.

"Suddenly a whim seizes him to turn pirate. He knows naught of the sea, cannot sail his own ship. But he buys a schooner, hoists what Francis Farrington Sprigg calls the Jolly Roger—which is a black flag bearing a death—and stands for the Spanish main to take all nations! Therefore, I say he must be mad."

"Holy angels," said I, "is this the escaped madman you sail to recover?"

He nodded: "Stede Bonnet and no other.... Well, Nancy, now that Mr. Eden is dead, where do you mean to go until Mr. Ross returns from the sea? Why do you not await him here at The Eden Arms until you can exchange 'em for Mr. Ross's arms?"

But I said I had a canoe and must be making sail for Charles-Town; and what he said about Mr. Ross madded me, and I would not listen to any advice from him, being, in my secret mind, determined to carry my bags of Arab gold into South Carolina, where was security and government, and there await the return of Mr. Ross.

So I had from the tavern a bag of hard bread, a cheese, some parched corn and sugar, a ham, and a cask of sweet water, all of which a servant carried to the water-stairs and stowed aboard the canoe.

Mr. Rhett, standing above and looking down, and a little tipsy, asked me why I had stowed aboard me all those little muddy sacks in a row.

"Ballast," said I, rudely.

"What kind?" asks he, laughing.

"Oh," said I, "the bags are full of hen's eggs and oysters. Or whatever your curiosity prefers," said I, with all the impudence in the world; "but the truth is," said I, "that they're full of Arab gold in bars, grains and dust, and lumps, worth £100,000. Will you marry such an heiress, Mr. Rhett?"

Which he seemed to think a great joke, for he laughed very heartily, balancing there on heel and toe, and a-blowing kisses at me.

So I hoisted my lateen and cast off the painter, and, blowing him a cat's kiss, stood for the inlet, scowling. "If you're lonely," called he, "send express for me to lay you aboard, my dear!"

Which vexed me, for my mind and heart were too full of Mr. Ross to jest lightly with other men. So I made him no answer.

Over the bar I saw Mr. Rhett's sloop beating up toward Edenton; and knew it had come to take him in pursuit of the escaped madman, Stede Bonnet.

I had a fair wind and sailed smartly before it southward; but, what between sad reflections concerning the desolate death of poor Mr. Eden, and my concern regarding Mr. Ross, who now had been some time at sea in chase of pirates, I was not in a very happy mood. Also, Mr. Rhett did vex me.

All afternoon I sailed; and, when it became dark, I landed, and ate a piece, and then slept in the canoe moored close inshore.

Morning broke fair and very warm, and I heard many land-birds singing on the dunes, although it was November.

All day long I sped southward before a light but constant wind, and that night I put into a creek where great trees overhung a beach of whitest sand and everywhere, in the early moonlight, mullet were jumping to catch stars.

Now, where I came ashore was an island. Others had been there before me, for I saw a broken cask and the ruins of a hut and a place where a fire had been made; but weeds grew among the ashes.

I was too tired to make a fire and cook, so I ate a bit of hard bread and some cheese, seated among trees a little way from the beach. It was deathly still in that place. A thin shroud of fog dimmed land and sea; and there was a gibbous moon, around which the mist spun a kind of ghostly glory.

Tall and spectral the trees rose against sea and sky, and no wind stirred them; and I heard no night-bird cry in the far silence, nor any sound only the making of the tide near to its flood.

Then, of a sudden, I was aware of a man moving between me and the sea.

He was pacing the strand in the foggy moonlight—a tall man in a full-bottomed wig, long laced coat, and boots; and his laced and feathered hat he carried in his hand.

When he came opposite to where I sat under a tree, he paused and looked toward me, and I could not doubt that he saw me.

But presently he moved on, tall, erect, and paced the sand as far as where the broken keg lay. Here he paused, and passed one hand over his shadowy face and brow, and pressed his fingers hard against his eyes, as though in perplexity.

Then back he strides along the seething edges of the tide, and stops again to look at me, and then, with bent head, on for a dozen paces. Now, again, he turns and back he comes; but this time bends his steps toward me, and I felt a slight chill of fear roughen my body and stir my hair.

When he came to where I sat I could see moonlight touching the pistols in his belt and shimmering along the gold lace and buttons of his sleeves; but his long face lay within the shadow of his wig, and the moon behind him made of his tall body a silhouette.

"Boy," said he in pleasant but hollow tones, "life is a sad and strange affair. In the end all find it so. It is because the brain grows old that the world ages and saddens."

I knew not what to say. He stood and passed a long, uncertain hand over his eyes, and over and over again, as though to clear his thought and vision.

Then he reached up and took off his long, heavily curled wig; and was a tall old bald man, or his head had been shaven for all that false brown hair.

"The human skull," says he in his hollow, cultivated voice, "should have a lid, so it could be lifted to cool the brain.... Boy, have you ever felt that your brain needed fresh, cool moonlight?"

"N-no, sir."

"Silvery, chilly moonlight? To cool and soothe the burning brain?"

"No, sir," I whispered.

He shook his head. "Life is a strange and dreary dream," said he. "Because the brain grows old.... Do you know the poets?"

"No, sir."

"I am one of them."

There was a silence, then he seated himself near me with a strange, stiff dignity of his mighty body.

"This," said he, "is a poem I have made. I will recite it to you for your pleasure and instruction." He lifted his long hand and beat time to accent the erratic rhyme; the cavernous mouth in his long horse-face opened. From it, in precise and fastidious accents, poured a kind of husky chant:

> "Now sounds the hour!
> Passes the power
> That Youth once flaunted;
> Wasted the dower
> That Love once vaunted;
> O God of sins untold,
> Which my dark mind have haunted,
> Fold upon fold,
> My brain grows old—
> That weary brain *she* taunted
> It was not gold I wanted!
> Thou knowest it was love, not gold.
> So, knowing, let Thy tall storm-cloud tower!
> Let ruin lower!—
> I stand undaunted."

As he ended a pale, infernal light played in his shadowy eyes, then went out like heat lightning which is as unreal as the false flame in the moon.

"I know not," said he in his husky, pleasant, and well-bred voice, "whether this poetry be good poetry or whether these unpruned lines might scan. I think that I am not a good poet. The world grows strange when the brain ages…. How old are you, my lad?"

"Seventeen, sir."

"Well then, love of woman is still a pretty word to you and not yet a passion. Nor is love of gold. No, not yet, my lad.... The world and the brain are born upon the same day. And are young together. And, together, grow old—old.... There is another love: the love of glory. But it is as vain as are all other loves and passions. Even the love of God."

He took a long horse-pistol from his sash and examined it.

"A medicine for aged brains," said he. "I wonder? ... Good medicine, perhaps, for fools. But that I am not—though some say I am a fool. And Black-Beard made me play the fool. So I sailed to pay him, but could not find him. And now he's dead. Which is the fool, my lad, the quick or dead? ... They're busy a-hanging many sea-rogues now. They hang 'em; then they gibbet them to swing and sun-dry.... And if the choked soul cling to the body, clutching it like a starved cat? I wonder.... It would be a dreary time for the soul while the body hangs in chains a-curing."

Chill after chill crawled over my body and through my hair as I looked at this tall old bald man in the foggy moonlight, a-playing with his pistol.

"Sir," said I in a small and fearful voice, "I do not follow all that you are pleased to say to me, but you seem to be unhappy."

"I have been that so long," said he, "that I would not know Happiness if I met her. Happiness is a nymph who plays sweetheart to you now and then. It has been a long time since she has quit my bed—this lovely light-o'-love."

He cocked his pistol and the sharp noise of the lock startled me. But he uncocked it, absently, and shoved it into his body sash. "No," he said to himself, "no."

Presently, looking up at me: "Happiness is a trull," said he in his husky, pleasant voice. "I sought her in the army. I became a major in his Majesty's guards. But I did not discover Happiness there. The jade had gone.

"I married a wife. And had children. I was possessed of wealth; I enjoyed the respect and friendship of men. But Happiness, whom I had thought to wed when I wedded my wife, proved unkind.

"Then it was that first my brain troubled me, and grew very, very old.... And the world, too, grew old around me.

"So I bought me a ship and a black flag. Perhaps I might find Happiness aboard a ship, thought ... And, to woo her, I determined to take all flags and all nations; and so I sailed On The Account in the Red Sea Trade. And flew a death and a bloody flag and a black pendant, too. To woo Happiness, when she came aboard me.... She never came.

"And, to woo and entice her, I took the *Anne of Glasgow*, and *The Endeavour* out of Bristol. And sixteen more vessels off Carolina between New York and Cape Fear—snows, pinks—and a Martinico man off Cape Henry and two snows off the Delaware.... In my ship *The Revenge*, schooner.... But Happiness would neither ship aboard me nor sign my articles.... And my brain and the world grew old and very gray and vague.... Boy, I had no need of money. I loved neither the sea nor ships; nor could I make sail or navigate a ship; but had a sailing-master to teach me. Yet, for all that, I am no fool. Only my brain is very restless what with age and pain and memories of what hath been and what has died.... Everything dies, my lad— even hate and love. And pain becomes a deadened pulse that only wearies."

He rubbed his eyes and brow for a while with his long fingers, then held up his great wig to air it in whatever wind was stirring.

Presently he put it on and arranged the thick brown curls on his shoulders. Then he clapped his laced and feathered hat upon his head.

"Boy," said he, "is that your canoe, yonder?"

"Yes, sir."

"Well," said he, "I have a pinnace in a cove not far away, and if I am not a fool I should go aboard and make sail. For," says he, "man's enemy—that hag whom we call Death—hath already offered me a bony and froward hand, which I refused. And lest she follow me here to make more free with me, I ought to hoist sail and stand for distant latitudes."

He rose with powerful grace and dignity and called out: "Harriott! I say Harriott! Have you filled the water-butt?"

The roar of a heavy musket answered him, and I saw the red flash of it among the trees.

I was on my feet instantly, and hid behind a tree; but he seemed dazed, and stood there in the foggy moonlight, passing his long fingers over his brow, gazing into darkness.

Out of it ran toward him a dozen men, the sparkle of moonlight on their weapons, and closed all around him, hedging in on him with naked swords.

Then came Mr. Rhett's voice: "I give you good quarters, Major Bonnet; but if you touch your pistols you are a dead man!"

Stede Bonnet stood rubbing his brow and his delicate, high-arched nose, and his large, prim mouth.

Then he took off his hat to Mr. Rhett and made him a leisurely and courtly bow.

So the man-o'-war's men came to him and took the pistols from his sash and the sword out of its sheath, and then tied his wrists in front of him with his own body scarf.

"Any more or your company except Harriott here?" inquired Mr. Rhett.

"No, sir. Did your shot kill poor Harriott?"

"He ran. We shot him," said Mr. Rhett coolly.

"Dead?"

"Quite."

"Well," said Major Bonnet with pleasant composure, "it's a strange world, Mr. Rhett, and has grown very old since I was a lad in England.... Have they tried any of my company in Charles-Town since my escape from prison?"

"All have had fair trial."

"The verdict?"

"All condemned save four."

"Which were they who have been found not guilty?" asked Bonnet gravely.

"Nicholas, Rowland Sharp of Bath-Town, Clark of Charles-Town and Tom Gerrard of Antegoa."

"And Bob Tucker?"

"Hanged."

"Neddy? Timberhead? Jim Rattle?"

"All hanged."

"On what charge?"

"Piracy. The *Francis* and the *Fortune* affairs."

"Is that the charge against me?" asked Bonnet pleasantly.

"It is."

"Very well, sir; let us go to meet it, then," said Major Bonnet calmly.

I saw them move away along the beach, Stede Bonnet's tall figure towering among them—dread and ghostly silhouettes against a gibbous moon which hung like a hump-back spider in a vast web of mist.

Then, at the water's edge, where a shallop was riding, I saw one of the man-o'-war's men pick up an oar; and he carried it before Mr. Bonnet. And—oh, God!—the moon silvered it, and it seemed to be the Silver Oar which is carried in the death-march to the gallows before all men condemned for piracy. And I knew that this man was doomed to die.

They say that he was hanged in his wig; and that when the cart started and the rope choked him, his full-bottomed, curly brown wig fell off, and left a tall, bald old man a-hanging there with his long hands tied in front of him, and his glazing eyes fixed on the horsemen saluting him with poised pikes.

For there is Government in South Carolina—just, they say—and both capable and severe.

And it is a strange world at best; but a young world, still, to me— like my heart which is very young, and was the world's twin when both were born.

CHAPTER XI
A YOUNGER SON

If there was no law in North Carolina there was plenty in South Carolina—what with Nicholas Trott in gown and wig, and Governor Johnson, and Colonel Rhett; and what with their Vice-Admiralty and their hanging and condemning and acquitting.

No! That was no place for me who had been taken twice in piracy—no place for me with my little bags of Arab gold where, by some process and colour of laws I never heard of, my fortune—which had been my father's lawful booty—would be taken from me and given to his Majesty and to his station-ships in the James.

And that I did not mean to suffer if I could help it; so, in the foggy light of a hateful and deformed moon, I hoisted my lateen and beat up toward the only haven I knew which was Topsail Inlet.

All night long I sailed, half asleep and dreaming of drowned men; half awake, and thinking of hanged men. And all the while, asleep or awake, I was neat to weeping, and vaguely conscious that I was in love and wanted my lover.

Oh, Lord, what a world had I been born into, where roguery had honesty by the throat, and where a gentleman might take a mistress below his station, but never a wife unless her fortune condoned his degradation!

So, with tender or with bitter thoughts, and with restless dreams of death and gallows, I sailed on, beating to the north-westward like a wind-baffled bird till the red dawn surprised me.

Out of half-awakened spray-drenched eyes I saw a reddened ocean and redder sky, and two ships at sea—a schooner and a sloop—and the sloop chased the schooner.

Within a mile of her she hoisted a black pennant, and the schooner instantly returned the compliment with an English ensign at mast-head and a gun to confirm it, making the best of her way and crowding all the sail she could.

The sloop, doing the like, hoisted a black flag with a death on it and fired her bow-chase, the schooner replying with her stern-chase out of her cabin windows.

I could see shot strike the sloop's gunnel and rigging, and tear through her sails; and one cut her fore-shroud on the starboard side and another her mast where it had been fished and was weak.

I was so near in my canoe that the roar of the sloop's guns and crash of splinters aboard her made my ears ache; and the round-shot flew through the wave-crests all around me, sending up jets like spouting fountains.

But the sloop was done for as far as any further chasing was concerned; for another shot hit the weakened mast and down it came carrying everything aloft, and lay overboard; and the pirate sloop careened to larboard so that I thought she would roll over and capsize.

Now came yells and curses and bawling and calling aboard her, and a loud racket of axes to clear away the wreckage.

Beating up past her I heard the sea-rogues damning and swearing; but some laughed at their own misfortune; and a great, half-naked fellow hailed me derisively from her wrecked fore-port:

"Canoe ahoy! We've struck to you, my boy, so for Jesus' sake give us good quarters!"

They took me for a poor fisherman with not a penny worth o' plunder aboard me. And I had £100,000 in Arab gold!

I was horribly afraid. I passed so near that I could see them salvaging what sail they dared and rigging a spar for a jury-mast— all amid a most horrid uproar of cursing and laughter and vile language.

Then, as I bore to starboard to cross her bows on a north-east tack, one of the rogues fired his pistol at me and roared with laughter to see me duck my head.

Such wanton wickedness enraged me and I stood up in the stern of my cockleshell and swore at the wretch.

Then I saw a lank, dandified officer come mincing across the high poop which was the sloop's quarter-deck, and look at me through a spy-glass. I knew him instantly, and my hair rose with fright, for he was Francis Farrington Sprigg.

"That's Tom Cocklyn's brat of a girl who plays the tap-boy at Topsail Inlet!" he said in his shrill, penetrating voice. "Clear the fore-port larboard gun!"

I gave myself up. It seemed a year before the loud crack of the gun followed and I felt the wind of the rushing round-shot whistling overhead. Far away a jet of foam burst upward out of the sea.

They fired two or three shots from muskets at me; to no purpose. No more shots came, as I tacked to leeward and to windward with all the desperation of a chased rabbit; and I think they had enough to do aboard them without contriving further mischief for a frightened girl in a cockleshell.

But it was like the cruelty of Francis Farrington Sprigg to so use the helpless, for his wickedness and heartless abuse of those who fell into his clutches was well known and common talk in taverns. Besides, Francis Farrington Sprigg had been quartermaster to Ned Low, the cruellest sea-rogue who ever flew the bones; and when Low had taught him all the wickedness he knew, he stole a ship from him to sail elsewhere and learn more of Captain Death.

Well, I made for the land which now began to be familiar to me; and there was an inlet very near which my canoe could enter even at low tide, and which led into endless links of creek and bay and lagoon and sound, and by devious and shallow reaches to the sea; and so into Topsail Inlet.

When I entered this creek I could make out the rover sloop now beating up under jury rig; but I knew she could never follow where I was sailing.

Sometimes I poled; sometimes rowed; then hoisted sail again and stood away across some windy bay or inland stretch of shallow water.

Once these dunes and shores were populated by fishermen and seafaring folk; but the dreadful Tuscarora war had made a desolation of all this region. Only into Old Clarendon had returned a few strange, slinking folk of whom wayfarers were more afraid than of the savages.

Now, for a long while, the seaward dunes had hid ocean from my view. It was afternoon by the sun, and near two o'clock. So I beached my cockleshell and ate and drank and lay flat on my aching back to recover strength to go on.

But before I set sail I ran to the seaward dunes and took a good look around.

The sloop, still under jury rig, sailed slowly northward. The schooner was not to be seen.

So, well content, I ran to my canoe and made sail once more, and, because the wind had shifted to the south-west made good progress.

Again and again in the open sounds I fell asleep at the helm, but always seemed to know when to awake.

The last time I awoke I was at sea, and flying before a brisk little wind with Topsail off of my larboard quarter and the sunset kindling behind the pines.

Oh, holy angels, how content was I to be there as my canoe went dashing through the inlet to Tom Cocklyn's landing.

Against the crimson west the old Lost Ship Tavern stood stark and drear; and if anybody were within I could not tell, because there was no light in any window.

But food and fitful sleep and a sense of safety had heartened and refreshed me. I moored my canoe, shipped mast, furled sail, and, making all fast, ran across the dunes to the kitchen door.

When I came to it I saw it was open, and smelled bacon a-broiling. Oh, heavenly angels, how sweet a smell! Yet was I cautious and peeped into the kitchen; and there saw Moll Fair a-squatted on the hearth and baking ash-cakes while bacon broiled and a kettle sang upon the hob.

I do not violently love that wench, but now I spoke her name with a loud sob; and when she got to her naked feet with a cry of "Lawks!" and a staring eye, why, I embraced and kissed the pretty slattern— but presently desisted because she returned my caress too ardently to suit me. Then a torrent of topsy-turvy discourse burst out of her red lips:

"Freckles," says she, "you are a heartless lad to leave me here alone so long with naught to do save to eat and sleep, and not a soul in breeches has come near this accursed place save only that old hoot-owl, Mr. Justice Nicholas Trott, Esqre, and may the devil's dam sit on his chest to warm his heart if it can be warmed at all— for the old scratch-wig regarded me sourly and reproached me because I ate and drank what belonged to Government, and I merely caretaker to impounded and sequestered property under the laws of Carolina— My God, is a caretaker not to eat and drink? What does that old buzzard live on himself, I'd like to ask him? And what does he think a young and healthy woman is nourished on to keep life in her toiling body—"

I took hold of her and shook her:

"Be quiet!" I cried, stamping my foot, "for I'm near dead o' my voyage and have more to do yet ere I make friends with a bed."

"I'll brew you a noggin," says she.

"No," said I, "I want a spade and a lantern; and when I return I'll eat a piece if I'm not too dead to open my mouth."

So she went out to the garden and fetched me a spade and a lantern; and lit the candle for me with splinter-wood.

With these I ran back to the dunes and fell to digging a pit ten paces due east of a pine—just a little shallow pit where I might hide my sacks of gold until I had slept and rested and refreshed myself sufficiently to dig a deeper and more secret pit in some safely concealed place, on the morrow.

Very soon I had made a hole quite deep enough. Now I hastened to unload my canoe; and was like to drop in my tracks of weariness before I had fetched every sack and covered all with sand.

When again I came to the kitchen I was too much fatigued to eat, so crept up to my attic bed and there fell upon it and slept all dressed and wet with spray and perspiration as I was.

All that night I slept and all the next day; and when I awoke it was already another sunset which flamed like a forest of pitch pine afire, reddening sea and land.

I stripped off my clothes, and went to the attic window and looked out upon a scene of fiery solitude; nothing stirred on land or sea, not even a gull.

I stepped, naked, into my shoes—for the puncheon floor was rough—and, flinging a ragged blanket around my body, descended to the kitchen.

Moll Fair lay asleep in the chimney corner, a fragment of ash-cake in her greasy fingers.

Fire smouldered on the hearth; the kitchen was very hot and smelled of burned fat. The outer air, too, seemed warm as midsummer. I went out very silently and took the spade from the pig-yard, and, thence, made my way through the still, ruddy afterglow, to that same dune where I had hid my Arab gold the night before.

Measuring ten paces from the solitary pine, I drove in my spade, left it upright, and ran down to the shore where a heavy tide was already making.

Here I stepped from my shoes, dropped the blanket, and hastened into the water to cleanse me of the dirt and sweat of many days.

Like a wild waterfowl I doused my yellow head; dipped and soused and scrubbed it with both hands; and used the fine, white velvet sand on my body. Shoulder deep I waded here and there or swam about, with ever a wild bird's eye on guard when I came to the surface.

All colour had gone from sea and sky; the Rogue's Moon had a belly and rode the fleece like tipsy Bacchus; and the black pine-tops stirred with the warm land-winds rising to welcome their sister breezes from the sea.

On my blanket I dried myself, slipped my feet into the shoes, and ran up to the landward dune where my spade stuck.

Angels divine! it was heavy work to dig out my little sacks of gold and then descend into the shallow pit and throw out damp sand.

Perspiration bathed me and I cast off the blanket and worked only in my loosened shoon.

Down, down I dug, until the excavation was shoulder deep. Then

I climbed out, and cast in my bags of gold, counting them one by one.

For a while I stood breathing in the fresh sea-wind to cool me, then I bent my back to shoveling in all the sand that I had heaved out.

When at last I had accomplished this and had smoothed it all as best I could, I found a fallen pine bough and dragged this to and fro over the spot.

And now I covered me with my blanket once more and carried the spade to the hog-yard.

Moll still snored in the kitchen, her pretty, over-flushed face cradled in her loosened hair; and a quart measure beside her, empty—which was why her face glowed like a cabbage-rose, I think.

When, in the attic, I had dressed me in the boy's clothes given me by Mr. Ross, I came again to the kitchen to get me a sup of buttery beer and a bit of cheese.

Moll opened one eye and looked at me.

"You've slept the clock around," she murmured; and went to sleep again.

Now I had scarce finished a few crumbs and tipped the tankard skyward when I heard a man in the yard and saw a light; and, thinking instantly I had been spied upon while a-burying my gold, I ran into the taproom and, from over the fireplace, unhooked a pair of Tom Cocklyn's brass horse-pistols which I knew he had left primed and loaded.

Now, hearing somebody at the front door, I did not go there but slipped around by the kitchen, and out, and came up behind a man who carried a lighted lantern and who was a-knocking upon the tavern door.

"What do you want?" said I, which gave him a start.

But when be turned to face me I saw he was a man-o'-war's man, and his cutlass hung at his side and his pistol stuck snug in his belt.

"Well," says he, "whose regiment of artillery are you, with six yard of horse-pistols in both fists?"

I was ashamed, and muttered that these were unsteady times in a lonely tavern.

"Where's Freckles, the tap-boy?" says he.

"Who asks for him?" said I, frightened.

"Mr. Ross, if you must know."

"Oh," said I in heavenly relief, "I am the tap-boy. Where is Mr. Ross?"

He pointed to the inlet. "We carry no riding lights, being in chase," says he. "Mr. Ross desires a word with you aboard the *Moth*."

So I ran back to lay aside my horse-pistols, and came to him again. And so to the beach where was a cockle, and three mariners to row us to the *Moth*.

The sloop-tender lay not far out, the bar being deep in flood and the tide still making.

Up and over I climbed, my heart a wild tumult and my eyes aching to see this man who, Mr. Rhett said, was one of those gentlemen that did not marry beneath them.

The officer of the watch on deck sent me below. The cabin door stood open and there I saw Mr. Ross in the lantern light—angels of God, he was a bonnie sight to see!

"Freckles!" he exclaims, jumping up and coming to me with arms extended.

Oh, holy angels, I walked into them with no other thought than that I desired to; and held up my face for the kiss upon my mouth which he never yet had offered, though I think designed to bestow upon me on several occasions.

Now, would you believe me that this great fool kissed only my two cheeks like a doddering granddad? I was so vexed that tears started, and I knew not whether to kiss him by main force or kick and slap him. I did neither, but sat down beside him on his table's edge upon the papers he had been a-conning; and instantly my mouth overflowed with words, and continued to pour them out until I had told him everything. Excepting only that I had discovered my father's fortune of £100,000.

"Nancy," said he, "I have thought about you every hour since I last saw you and always, when ashore, have sought news of you and how it went with Topsail, and if the sequestered property had been sold by the Courts."

"No," said I; "Judge Trott came once to scold Molly for eating too freely of Government stores."

We both laughed.

"Why are you here?" I asked, taking a firmer hold of his hand which held mine more firmly still.

"Why," said he, "I'm in chase of Francis Farrington Sprigg, who hath left a very bloody wake northward from Canaveral. Eighteen sail, Freckles! And everywhere most wanton murder. Why, he locked under hatches half a hundred poor negroes in a Guinea man's bold; and there were horses aboard; and among these he drove master and crew and then set fire to the ship."

Wickedness so terrible bewildered me, and I trembled to remember my encounter with this human devil the day before.

Said Mr. Ross: "No doubt he sails without lights; but if he still carried jury rigging then I ought to come to him very soon.

"I thought he might be hanging around Lost Ship Tavern. There's been some rumours of buried treasure since they hanged Tom Cocklyn. But," he added, "there always is such gossip when any sea-rogue dies air-dancing."

"What rumours, sir?"

"Why, it's said that Tom Cocklyn was quartermaster aboard some pirate who took near £100,000 in Arab gold out of a tall ship, merchant; and that the two of them buried it near Topsail; and that Francis Farrington Sprigg had this for certain from a man in Charles-Town who knew Jack Ketch; and that Jack Ketch had it from Tom Cocklyn in exchange for enough rum to make him drunk at the gallows."

"Do you believe it?"

"No. I think old Tom lied at the tree. Nevertheless, if Francis Farrington Sprigg believes it, he may come here and start a-digging."

"Mr. Ross," said I, "if a poor girl be humbly born, yet hath in her own right a fortune, would a gentleman think to marry her?"

"That's an odd question, Nancy," said he, smiling.

"Is it odd, sir?"

"Well, no. I'll answer it by saying that gentlemen have married beneath their quality for such a reason. And, now and then, for love alone, also."

"But that, seldom?"

"Seldom."

"So a poor girl need hope for no churching from a gentleman?"

"Usually they seem to be content without it."

"And those few who are not content to live in love without a wedding ring. What of them, sir?"

"Well," said he, "they have their reward, haven't they?"

"You say so…. And the man goes elsewhere? Is that it?"

"Sometimes, Nancy."

"Well," said I, "it's an odd world, and a strange and sad one—as poor Stede Bonnet had it—and what love really is I never shall guess, I think…. Only that if it be the undoing of anyone, then it cannot be love—let them call it what they please—"

The quartermaster's startled voice at the door: "Sir, a great ship in the dark on our weather bow and murder being done aboard her!"

Mr. Ross sprang from the table and I ran after him on deck. As he mounted the poop, I at his heels, from the deck of an unseen ship a cable's length away rose a sheet of fire from a flare, lighting the most horrible scene that ever I have witnessed.

For there, close to us, in the lurid glare, lay a great ship, drifted so close that we could almost have lashed and laid her aboard, and on the swarming deck I saw a huge man all bloody like a devil; and he had the ship's captain on a hatch and had opened his body alive and was trying to pull out his guts whilst the wretch shrieked as he was drawn alive.

"My God!" shouted Mr. Ross, "what hell's vision is this!"

Already the great ship was all afire forward, which made all as red and clear as a violent sunset; and I saw Francis Farrington Sprigg turn from the torture and look over his shoulder at us so suddenly revealed riding almost aboard him without lights.

At that instant our hull rubbed against the ship and the spars grated and scraped our rigging till the taut shrouds sounded like ringing bow-strings.

"Lash her!" shouted Mr. Ross. "Cheerily, my bullies! Carry her by the board! Out pike and cutlass! Now, lads, for old England!"

As I scrambled over the rail amid a swarm of sailors, I caught a glimpse in the spreading redness around me, of Sprigg's sloop warped in close to the great ship, and her jury rigging alone to carry her.

I had no weapon but took a belaying pin on my way, and instantly was in a crowd of our man-o'-war's men carrying all before them with pike and cutlass.

The poor murdered wretch on the hatch fell to the deck, gushing out his life with a last gasp. The wretch who had used him alive like an executioner turned to run, but slipped in his victim's blood and fell sprawling. And one of our bullies sheared off his head with a broad-axe.

This sickened me who have only a girl's stomach at best, and I took hold of the ship's rail and was sick amid all that awful uproar and yelling and the pistolling and musketry and clash of hangers and pikes.

Over into their own sloop tumbled the pirates; nor could our own men endure the flames which now raged forward and burst from the great ship's waist; and the thick smoke and stench of tar and turpentine warned us of her cargo and to quit her while we could.

I heard Mr. Ross warning our men aboard us, and the crew of the merchant, too, lest the lashings be cut before they could make us.

Seeing me with my belaying pin: "Get you aboard, you little fool!" he cried in a rage. "Great God, must I turn nurse to you that you break not that yellow noddle!"

So I climbed aboard the *Moth* among a swarm of our men and all others of the merchant's crew who were left alive upon the great ship's deck; and when all were aboard, and the lashings cut, we made out to fall clear of the doomed ship, dropping astern of her. And there, in the lurid glare, I read her name—the *Evening Star*, of Leith.

Now, as we dropped astern of the *Evening Star*, which was all afire, the sea-rogues' sloop was unmasked under her miserable jury rigging.

Never have I looked upon such an evil thing as seemed this wicked, crippled sloop to me. And I saw Francis Farrington Sprigg upon her poop a-mincing about in the light of the great ship's flames like a dandy dawdling through hell.

Mr. Ross hailed him.

"Oh, go to the devil," said he, "and be damned to you"; and I heard him ordering the sloop's after-guns to swing and bear on us.

"Will you take good quarters?" shouted Mr. Ross.

"Will you mind your own damned business?" replied Francis Farrington Sprigg.

"Sink him," said Mr. Ross.

A clap of thunder from our broadside and a vast bank of crowding vapours behind which our guns were run in, sponged, loaded, primed, and the port-fires dashed to the breeches all at the gunner's signal.

Then, beyond the sheet of fire lashing out into the cannon mist, and our ship trembling with the broadside's shock to her very keel, I saw the pirate vomit out a vast fountain of fire, and a stunning concussion staggered me.

All over us rained brands and burning flakes. A huge pall of smoke mounted to hide the pot-bellied Rogue's Moon.

When my sense of hearing returned to me I heard Mr. Ross saying that the pirate's magazine had blown up, and that there was an end to Francis Farrington Sprigg.

In the raging red light of the great ship afire, Mr. Ross came from the bittacle to where I stood.

"Freckles," said he, "are you hurt?"

"No, sir. Are you?"

Then he took me by the shoulders, and so, into his arms. I held down my head, but he lifted it and kissed my mouth. And I suffered it as a blessed soul suffers the first bliss of Paradise.

CHAPTER XII
NANCY TOPSFIELD

All night long the great ship burned off Topsail Inlet. I did not see it, for I lay asleep on my trundle in the attic. Complete exhaustion of mind and body made my sleep so deep and dreamless that the eastern sun spread the window's pattern over my bed when I unclosed my dazzled eyes.

It was not the sun that awoke me, but Moll Fair's voice at my door:

"Freckles!" she bawls, and: "Freckles, would you sleep till resurrection!"

I saw her at the garret door gazing at me, and her large doe-eyes of a heavy feeder a little wild.

"Freckles," says she; "there is a sea-chest sent ashore for you in the taproom, and Mr. Ross sends word he will come ashore to wait upon you at noon. Oh, Freckles, are you a *girl?*"

I sat up in my ragged cotton shift.

"Lawks!" she screams, "it is God's truth!" She began to cry and I to laugh; and, "Oh, Freckles!" she sobs, "when I have waited only for you to notice me!—and showed you tenderness—and you've made a fool of me, you jade—"

"Will you stop your blubbering?" said I, still laughing. "What the devil are you bawling for who have fetched me many a kick and slap and pinch—"

"Because I loved you—boo-hoo—" says she; whereat I fell back upon my bed a-squirm with laughter.

But presently remembering the message from Mr. Ross, and the sea-chest, I hopped out o' bed, and, putting on my shoes, ran down to the taproom.

Molly came shuffling after me, sniffling, digging at her tear-wet eyes with her mottled knuckles.

"Here," says she, "is a letter from Mr. Ross for you—you false minx! And here is the key he sent—"

I snatched the letter and bade Molly open the chest whilst I was a-reading:

FRECKLES,

I send you a sea-chest full of female apparel taken from the pirate, Sam Kreech, off Cape Fear where we destroyed him. As Kreech had plied the Red Sea Trade, we discovered only Barbary finery aboard him; so this is the best I am able to do for you until I can carry you to Charles-Town where women's apparel may be purchased suitable for your youthful years and civilized condition.

I shall come ashore to wait upon you at noon.

JOHN ROSS.

I turned and looked into the chest which Molly had unlocked and opened, and from which she was wildly pulling silks and embroideries.

"Gentle angels!" said I, "does he wish me to dress like a bashaw's daughter that he sends me a chest of garments such as these?"

But at the sight of so much finery the pretty slattern had gone quite mad, for she seized one garment after another to drape them against her person with delighted squeals, and strutted to and fro with silks and satins a-fluttering about her like a popinjay at a country frolic.

There was a little jacket like a vest, with designs of an Arab nature in gold upon a ground of turquoise-blue silk. This and a full white shift of ivory-tinted silk I seized, and the short white skirt to match it.

Shoes, too, with upturned toes from which dangled tiny gold tassels, I discovered, but no stockings; so concluded that the bashaw's daughters wore none.

When I had dressed in these, Moll fetched me a sash striped with turquoise, pale orange and green, and I girdled my body with this under the little jacket.

There had been a mirror in the tavern, but Edward Teach's men had broken it with pistol shots the day they robbed the till. However, I had a fragment of it, and Moll held it before me, raising and lowering it so I could view myself.

"Lawks," says she, "you are a pretty thing in heathen garments, though in English apparel you are like to seem somewhat plain—what with your clipped yellow hair of a boy and several freckles—"

"Why shall I take thought for my face," said I, "if it does well enough to suit the man to whom it matters?"

"Oh, la," says she a-simpering, "do you mean Mr. Ross?"

"Him or another or the next who bids me good morning," said I gaily. "For I'll tell you this, Molly: the world is very full of handsome young men who seem willing to prove kinder than a young girl finds necessary.

"If I should tell you how many I saw in Charles-Town and Edenton, and not counting those aboard ships—why, you would find it very difficult to believe me."

"I would to God," she pouted, "that I might have of these silken garments enough to dress me like a daughter of the Grand Mogul."

"Choose," said I, happily, "and play the Sheba Queen with me."

She chose a scarlet vest and a green and gold shift, and trousers of green which seemed very beautiful but barbarous. She gave me a crimson handkerchief with which to bind my head, which I did; and she knotted a yellow and red one around her own unkempt locks, which made us both look like sea-rogues in the Red Sea Trade.

Well, we cooked a breakfast for us, careful to spatter nothing upon our rich clothing; but it seemed strange to sit in the chimney and eat ashen cakes and bacon from a beachen dish and pull at our pewters instead of quaffing Canary out of golden goblets.

"Devil take me," said she, "—to think I am only a kitchen queen at best. If I had ten pounds I know a man-o'-war's apprentice aboard Sir George Sayles who would marry me."

"What would he do if you had five hundred pounds, Molly?" I asked, seriously.

"Rather say, what would *I* do!"

"Well, what?"

"Marry the man I love."

"Who is that?"

"Dick Langley, boatswain aboard Sir George."

"Would he ring and church you for five hundred pounds?"

"And for twenty-five pounds. He hath said it. But lawks-a-lassie, Freckles, where shall he find twenty-five pounds who cannot save a stiver of his pay? And where am I to find it who have not a groat to drop into my stocking—and no stocking either!—no, not these twelve-month, for Tom Cocklyn took mine that I had knitted me and gave me a box on the ear to pay me."

And so we sat in the kitchen a-gossiping and eating and drinking buttery beer.

Out o' the open door where the hens wandered and peeped in at us and made a great feathered rush when we flung 'em a crust, I could see Mr. Ross's ship, the *Moth*, sloop-tender to Sir George Sayles's station-ship, *Sea-Hawk*, lying snugly at her anchor; and men aloft to mend spars and rigging, and men on deck a-sewing up rents in sails where some sea-rogues' fire had done damage.

Half a mile astern of her lay the great ship—burned to the water's edge and lodged upon the bar. Only her charred ribs showed, and the stump of her mizzen, with a great mass of blackened wreckage on her larboard quarter, and thousands of gulls flying about her.

As for the rover-vessel of Francis Farrington Sprigg, not a shred or splinter remained of captain, crew, or ship, who had sailed nearer to God, upon that hell's blast from her magazine, than ever they were likely to attain again.

I could see sharks' fins a-plenty shearing the water, which doubtless had been bloody enough the night.

Moll told me that when the pirate blew up she had been sitting upon the threshold of the kitchen door to watch the fight; and eating of a bit of cheese.

"I could see a man going up upon a shaft of fire," said she, "and his arms and legs waving crazy; and down he comes, and over and over like a spin-wheel, splash in the red glare. And, oh, God, the water whirled in a great eddy around him and a shark played and played with him—"

"That's enough," said I with a shudder.

"Yes, I could not finish my cheese," said she, picking out another ash-cake and laying upon it a strip of bacon.

Thus, as I say, we conversed, until the sun seemed very close to noon; and, in a little while, I perceived the ship's longboat making for the inlet.

The happy tumult in my breast became almost unendurable with confusion and the apprehension born of self-distrust. I ran to look at myself in the fragment of the taproom mirror; I washed my face and hands in a bucket of soft water. Oh heaven, what freckles I had who never before had considered them—two pale ones on my nose, and several upon my cheeks.

As for my hair, combing did not help that curly tangle, so I let it go and be damned to it; and ran out and down across the dunes where John Ross was just stepping ashore.

When he saw me in my Barbary silks he laughed and took off his laced and feathered hat, and, coming to where I stood, kissed my hand with charming malice yet tenderest respect. Had I not been in love with him I had instantly loved him then.

Now he gave me his hand and carried me across the dunes by the wharf path to the tavern, conversing with every ceremony and politeness; saying that my clothing made me charming, and that a bit of Barbary did me no wrong.

"For," says he, mischievously, "there is some little of barbarity in you anyway, Nancy Topsfield, and I think Herodiade might have resembled you."

Said I: "Have I ever demanded your head, St. John?"

"Ah," says he, "St. John is better than *Sir* John or 'my lord.'"

"How would Saint Jack do, sir?"

We laughed together under the high blue sky as we slowly crossed the dunes and came to The Lost Ship Tavern.

"Will you be pleased to enter, sir?" said I.

"Let us sit together here upon this green settle in the sun."

So we seated ourselves upon Tom Cocklyn's old green settle, under the taproom window, where that sea-rogue used to sit with his spyglass sweeping the ocean for sails.

"Nancy," said Mr. Ross, "the Court of Vice-Admiralty hath judged my prize. Have you heard so?"

"Yes, sir."

"You mean, 'yes, John?'"

"Yes—John."

"Have you heard, also, that all is in order, and the seizure justified?"

"Yes."

"Yes—what?"

"Yes—Jack."

"Darling!" he said under his breath; and so heavenly a shaft pierced my breast that I lost breath and came suddenly near to tears.

So he took hold of my hand, and I held to his as tightly, and for a little while we remained silent there in the November sunshine, looking blindly out to sea.

"Well," said he, "I am a wealthy man—or shall be—when I have my prize money."

After a silence: "What is a poor girl to think of you now—my lord?"

"You little devil," said he between his teeth.

"I am no devil. But—I *am* Nancy Topsfield."

"I know that, too."

"Daughter of Captain Topsfield—my lord—"

"If you say it but once again I kiss your mouth—here, in full view of every spy-glass aboard the *Moth*!"

I said nothing.

"Nancy; are you contented to see me a wealthy man?"

"Oh," said I, "as far as churching is concerned, I had married you though you had no more than the clothes to your back.... If that is what you mean. Do you?"

He looked at me soberly and said in a low voice: "Did you think I did not mean to marry you, Nancy Topsfield?"

I turned hot and confused at that:

"M-Mr. Rhett s-said—" I stammered, "that gentlemen seldom married beneath their q-q-quality."

"Did he say that to you?"

"Yes—"

"In argument, I suppose," he added drily, "to pave a way to further persuasion."

"No; he was kind, but a trifle kindled with the wine we drank—"

"You and Rhett?"

I gave him a swift look, and could have laughed and cried aloud my pleasure in the scowl he wore.

"You are a devil," said he, "but I believe an honest one."

"You may believe it—my lord—"

At that I was in his arms before I could resist, and he kissed my mouth, and held me, and kissed me again and again. And under God knows how many spy-glasses from that ship across the dunes!

Well, I was paid for my impudence.

"My darling," said he, "who doubted that I truly was in love with her who gave me my life and honour and made of me a man who had been a fool, a gambler and a sot, and ready to turn rogue—"

At that I gave him a very tender look and told him I had liked him even when I thought him a rogue.

"But," said I, "how could the daughter of Captain Topsfield do other than she did that dreadful night?"

"Not otherwise. No. And—do you remember that I made my manners to you as though you had been the equal of any?"

"Yes. And I loved you for it upon that instant."

"You say it to please me—"

"No, I fell in love at that instant. I did not so regard it, then. Later I knew."

"Well," said he, "it is God's mercy on me that I came to The Lost Ship to meet Captain Death. Else, in this hour, I had hung a-sun-drying on Execution Dock or my fragments had spattered the sea along with the dismembered carcass of Francis Farrington Sprigg."

After a pause: "Sir—" I began—from habit—and partly from

reverence and love; but he made an end to it for good and all, so:

"Jack, dearest," said I, blushing brightly at the heavenly liberty, "I wonder what I am to bring you who do me this happy honour to ask of me my hand, having my heart already in your power."

"Sweetheart," says he, "have I not told you that the Vice-Admiralty Court makes me rich?"

"Whither do you sail when you weigh from here?" I asked.

"To Charles-Town with you. To marry you," said he with calm deliberation more stirring than a storm of passion.

Oh, heavenly angels, how he was thrilling me with every look and breath and word!

"John Ross," said I, "would it please your pride and soothe it to marry one who also might bring to you a fortune?"

He smiled at that: "Not a whit," said he. "My pride is nowise bruised whose very source hath sprung anew from you."

"My God, sir, you are sixth son to the Earl of Cardross."

"And if I were the King's son, and had become the rogue I meant to be, where lies the honour save in her who preserved it?"

I began to cry, still looking at him but making no great noise, only with some gulping and sniffing and the tears following one another to course down beside my freckled nose.

Well, he kissed me several times, not considering the glass aboard the *Moth*, nor the man-o'-war's men on the beach below.

"John," said I, "my father took from a Barbary rogue several grass-sacks of Arab gold in flakes, grains, dust, lumps and bars, to the value of £100,000."

When he recovered from his astonishment he begged me gently not to think on it anymore because he would have ample fortune for us both.

Then, putting my lips to his ear, I whispered to him the truth; and I could see how amazement and incredulity meddled with his belief.

"There is a spade," said I, "in the hog-yard. Call up two men and let them uncover what I have buried so that we may carry it into Charles-Town, and you have it of me in the hour we marry."

"In that hour," said he, "I shall not touch it; nor ever in any hour of any day or year. For it is yours, Nancy Topsfield—"

I fell to snivelling again. "Oh heaven," said I, "—when my only thought was that it might be yours one day—"

He kissed me and stood up to signal to his boat's crew with his laced hat. When they came, he sent the skiff-swain for the spade; then I took his hand and led him to the solitary pine tree, and, thence, measured ten paces east.

I kept tight hold of his hand, standing beside him in silence until he who was a-digging uncovered the first sack.

Then I unloosed his hand and ran to the tavern where Molly stood by the kitchen door a-watching everything in her gaudy silks of Barbary.

"Freckles," says she in flushed excitement, "does Mr. Ross mean to ring and church you?"

"Yes, and I him," said I laughing, and as excited as she.

"Lawks!" says she, "then you shall be, someday, Countess Cardross!"

"Never, I think," said I, "because five healthy brothers come first."

"Nevertheless," cried she, "there are wars and misfortunes and acts of God—"

I took hold of her and shook her plump shoulders till she quivered like a jelly.

"Be quiet!" said I, "and never again give shameful tongue to thoughts so base! Now, then, do you wish to care for me and be tire-maid to me, and so learn something of the arts of civilization? Yes or no?"

She said she did, in a bewildered way.

"Will you promise to keep your person very clean with soap?"

"Yes," said she, "if it be scented soap like that which Mr. Justice Trott carries in his saddle-bags for to wash his hands at a journey's end."

"Very well," said I; "make your packet, and you shall sail presently with me to Charles-Town. And I tell you this, Molly Fair: if you use me honestly, and not like a lazy slattern, in one year I endow you with five hundred pounds for to marry you lawfully to Dick Langley, your boatswain aboard Sir George Sayles."

Whereupon she would have kissed my hand but I gave her a hearty slap on the rump and bade her never act the fool toward me, and was near swearing at her only that I seldom swear.

"You frowsy baggage," said I, "fetch a bucket of sweet water and wash yourself, for we may have to sleep in company aboard the *Moth*." And so left her anxiously obedient and all a-twitter over prospect of happy fortune.

Standing there by the kitchen door in the sunshine, I could see Mr. Ross's men carrying my sacks to the boat.

I looked at the hens pensively picking around me; I looked at our hog who gave me a gentle grunt. There were horses, and three cows, also; and concerning these I must take thought before I left this ancient house.

As I stood there, a-thinking, I heard a gun at sea; and, looking up, saw cannon smoke clouding the *Moth*, and her ensign flying to confirm her gun.

For an instant sheer terror possessed me. Then I perceived a great ship coming in grandly out of the open sea, the Cross of St. George at her main and a broad pendant at her mizzen; and I knew her to be our station-ship, the *Sea-Hawk*, Sir George Sayles.

So I ran across the dune to Mr. Ross, and begged him to ask Sir George the loan of his boatswain until Government could send a person from Bath-Town to care for the tavern and the dumb creatures dependent upon man.

"Surely," said he, smiling; "and Sir George shall unite Moll Fair and her boatswain, if it pleases them.... And if it pleases *you*, Nancy Topsfield."

Happiness left me dumb.

"Shall we embark?" said he.

So I laid my hand upon his, and he kissed it, and so led me slowly across the dunes to the longboat awaiting us below.

THE END

ROBERT W. CHAMBERS BIBLIOGRAPHY

In the Quarter (1894)

The King in Yellow (1895; stories)

The Red Republic (1895)

With the Band (1896; poetry)

A King and a Few Dukes (1896)

The Maker of Moons (1896; stories)

The Mystery of Choice (1897; stories)

The Haunts of Men (1898; stories)

Ashes of Empire (1898)

Lorraine (1898)

Outsiders (1899)

Cambric Mask (1899)

The Conspirators (1900; UK as A Gay Conspiracy, 1900)

Cardigan (1901)

The Maid-at-Arms (1902)

The Maids of Paradise (1903)

In Search of the Unknown (1904)

A Young Man in a Hurry and Other Short Stories (1904)

The Reckoning (1905)

Iole (1905)

The Tracer of Lost Persons (1906)

The Fighting Chance (1906)

The Tree of Heaven (1907; stories)

The Younger Set (1907)

The Firing Line (1908)

Some Ladies in Haste (1908)

Special Messenger (1909)

The Danger Mark (1909)

Ailsa Paige (1910)

The Green Mouse (1910)

Adventures of a Modest Man (1911)

The Common Law (1911)

The Streets of Ascalon (1912)

Japonette (1912; serialized as *The Turning Point, Cosmopolitan,* 1914)

The Gay Rebellion (1913)

The Business of Life (1913)

Blue-Bird Weather (1913)

Quick Action (1914)

The Hidden Children (1914)

Anne's Bridge (1914)

Between Friends (1914; novelette)

Who Goes There! (1915)

Athalie (1915)

Police!!! (1915; stories)

The Better Man (1916; stories)

The Girl Philippa (1916)

Barbarians (1917; interconnected war stories)

The Dark Star (1917)

The Restless Sex (1918)

The Laughing Girl (1918)

In Secret (1919)

The Moonlight Way (1919)

The Crimson Tide (1919)

The Slayer of Souls (1920)

A Story of Primitive Love (1920; story)

The Little Red Foot (1921)

Eris (1922)

The Flaming Jewel (1922)

The Talkers (1923)

The Hi-Jackers (1923)

America, or the Sacrifice (1924)

Marie Halkett (UK: 1925; US: 1937; serialized as *The Jolly Roger, McCall's,* 1923-24)

The Girl in Golden Rags (UK: 1925;
    US: 1936)
The Mystery Lady (1925)
The Man They Hanged (1926)
The Way of Dionysia (1926; only
    published as *Red Book Magazine*
    serial)
The Drums of Aulone (1927;
    serialized as *The Fear of God*,
    Liberty magazine, 1926-27)
The Gold Chase (1927; serialized as
    "Thalassa!", *Cassell's Magazine*,
    1927)
The Rogue's Moon (1928)
The Sun Hawk (1928)
The Happy Parrot (1929)
Painted Minx (1930)
The Rake and the Hussy (1930)
Beating Wings (UK: 1930; US: 1936)
War Paint and Rouge (1931)
Gitana (1931; serialized as *Silver
    Knees*, *Liberty* magazine, 1931)
The Whistling Cat (1932)
Whatever Love Is (1933)
The Young Man's Girl (1934)
Secret Service Operator 13 (1934;
    UK as *Spy No. 13,* 1935; stories)
Love and the Lieutenant (1935)
The Fifth Horseman (1937)
Smoke of Battle (1938; completed by
    Rupert Hughes)

PLAYS/MUSICALS

The Witch of Ellangowan (1897; aka
    Meg Merrilies)
Iole (1913; musical comedy based on
    the novel)
Sintram and His Companions (opera
    libretto)

CHILDREN'S BOOKS

Outdoorland (1903)
Orchard-Land (1903)
River-Land (1904)
Forest-Land (1905)
Mountain-Land (1906)
Garden-Land (1907)